YOU BETTER RUN

EVA RAE THOMAS MYSTERY - BOOK 11

WILLOW ROSE

Cover design by Juan Villar Padron,
https://www.juanjpadron.com

Special thanks to my editor Janell Parque
http://janellparque.blogspot.com/

Join Willow Rose's VIP Newsletter to get exclusive updates about New Releases, Giveaways, and FREE ebooks.

Just scan this QR code with your phone and click on the link:

SCAN ME

Tired of too many emails? Text the word: "willowrose" to 31996 to sign up to Willow's VIP text List to get a text alert with news about New Releases, Giveaways, Bargains and Free books from Willow.

FOLLOW WILLOW ROSE ON BOOKBUB:

Connect with Willow online:
https://www.facebook.com/willowredrose/
https://twitter.com/madamwillowrose
http://www.goodreads.com/author/show
https://www.willow-rose.net
madamewillowrose@gmail.com

Books by the Author

HARRY HUNTER MYSTERY SERIES

- All The Good Girls
- Run Girl Run
- No Other Way
- Never Walk Alone

MARY MILLS MYSTERY SERIES

- What Hurts the Most
- You Can Run
- You Can't Hide
- Careful Little Eyes

EVA RAE THOMAS MYSTERY SERIES

- So We Lie
- Don't Lie to me
- What you did
- Never Ever
- Say You Love me
- Let Me Go
- It's Not Over
- Not Dead yet
- To Die For
- Such A Good Girl
- Little Did She Know
- You Better Run

EMMA FROST SERIES

- Itsy Bitsy Spider
- Miss Dolly had a Dolly
- Run, Run as Fast as You Can
- Cross Your Heart and Hope to Die
- Peek-a-Boo I See You
- Tweedledum and Tweedledee
- Easy as One, Two, Three
- There's No Place like Home
- Slenderman
- Where the Wild Roses Grow
- Waltzing Mathilda
- Drip Drop Dead
- Black Frost

JACK RYDER SERIES

- Hit the Road Jack
- Slip out the Back Jack
- The House that Jack Built
- Black Jack
- Girl Next Door
- Her Final Word
- Don't Tell

REBEKKA FRANCK SERIES

- One, Two...He is Coming for You
- Three, Four...Better Lock Your Door
- Five, Six...Grab your Crucifix
- Seven, Eight...Gonna Stay up Late
- Nine, Ten...Never Sleep Again

- ELEVEN, TWELVE...DIG AND DELVE
- THIRTEEN, FOURTEEN...LITTLE BOY UNSEEN
- BETTER NOT CRY
- TEN LITTLE GIRLS
- IT ENDS HERE

MYSTERY/THRILLER/HORROR NOVELS

- SORRY CAN'T SAVE YOU
- IN ONE FELL SWOOP
- UMBRELLA MAN
- BLACKBIRD FLY
- TO HELL IN A HANDBASKET
- EDWINA

HORROR SHORT-STORIES

- MOMMY DEAREST
- THE BIRD
- BETTER WATCH OUT
- EENIE, MEENIE
- ROCK-A-BYE BABY
- NIBBLE, NIBBLE, CRUNCH
- HUMPTY DUMPTY
- CHAIN LETTER

PARANORMAL SUSPENSE/ROMANCE NOVELS

- IN COLD BLOOD
- THE SURGE
- GIRL DIVIDED

My daddy's gotta gun – you better run

Hayloft, Mother Mother

There's a dead girl in the pool
I'm the dead girl in the pool

girl in red

Prologue

Cocoa Beach, Florida
8 a.m., Saturday morning

IT WAS a clear and humid morning in March, the day that Meg Kellam's world collapsed. From the minute she opened her eyes and blinked a few times to get the webs of the night out of them, she felt the deep dread rising inside her.

Empty bottles filled the coffee table before her, and soon she realized she was on the couch.

"I'm so thirsty," she mumbled and sat up, supporting her face with her hands, rubbing her forehead, and running a hand through her hair. The hand touched something sticky, and she pulled it out to look at it.

"Gum? How did I get gum in my hair? I must have laid on it while sleeping."

Meg pulled at it, and it got stuck between her fingers. She found an only slightly used napkin and wiped her fingers. Some of the gum came off, but her fingers still felt sticky, and she knew a big part of it was still in her hair.

She heard moaning from behind her and saw her best friend, Abbi, poke her head up from one of the other couches in her five-thousand-square-foot childhood home. The light coming in from the big glass sliding doors leading to the pool area blinded her slightly, and she held a hand up to cover her eyes.

"Heeeeyyy," Abbi said, her voice raspy. "How are you feeling?"

"Like someone threw up in my mouth," Meg said and stuck out her tongue.

Abbi groaned, exhausted. She looked at the small glasses lined up on Meg's mom's coffee table.

"Oh, God, we took shots before passing out, didn't we? Your mom would kill you if she saw that we weren't using coasters on her beloved coffee table," Abbi said, laughing. "Now, it's all covered in empty beer bottles and half-eaten chip bags."

Meg stared at the mess. Some of the chips had spilled onto the table and the carpet below; others had been soaked in spilled beer and were stuck to the glass top.

Meg opened her eyes widely.

"Mom," she said.

"What's that?" Abbi said, laughing. She sat up. Her hair was tousled. Abbi had the most beautiful long hair. Meg couldn't get hers as long since hers was fine and thin, another annoying trait she had probably inherited from her mother. At least she believed so.

"What time is it?" Meg asked anxiously. She threw a glance around the house. People were sleeping everywhere, even on the stairs... and so many empty bottles and something blue had spilled on the white carpet by the dining room table.

"It's only eight," Abbi said. "It's really early. We only slept like three hours. At least I think so, heh. I don't really remember passing out."

"My mom will be home in two hours," Meg said, shaking her head. "I knew I should never have let you talk me into having a party. There is no way we can clean up the house that fast."

"Hey, first of all, you wanted this party, not me. And of course, we can," Abbi said. "If we get everyone up and ask them to help. Don't worry. I'll make it happen."

Meg smiled, even though she still felt uneasy. Abbi got up from the couch and went to the kitchen. She came back with a box of trash bags, then clapped her hands.

"All right, everyone. Party is over. It's time to clean up. Wake up. Now!"

Meg was impressed with Abbi's persistence, and little by little, she succeeded in waking each and every person. Minutes later, they were all helping out, removing bottles and empty cans, wiping down counters and tables, and vacuuming the carpet. Soon, Meg started to breathe less raggedly and calmed down, thinking she was actually going to pull this off. They were going to make it.

"See?" Abbi said and came up to her. "We're almost done. Your

4

mom will never know you had a party while she was out of town. I promise."

Meg nodded, actually believing her. Until something outside the big sliding-glass windows caught her eye, and her heart stopped beating.

"THERE'S a girl in the pool. There's a girl in the pool!"

Meg stared through the window, pointing and clasping her mouth.

"What?" Abbi said and dropped the garbage bag in her hand. The contents clattered as it landed on the tiles. Abbi came up next to Meg, who could barely breathe. The words coming out of her mouth were spoken between ragged breaths.

"There's... a... girl...."

"What are you talking about? Meg, you look all pale; what is...?"

Abbi turned her head and looked out the window. She spotted the bobbing colorful lump at the bottom of the clear pool outside, then let out a slight gasp.

"Are you sure? It kind of looks more like... It could just be some clothes? Maybe someone threw clothes in the pool? Or maybe it's a doll?"

Meg shook her head. "No. I think it's...."

Abbi put a hand on her shoulder. "Let's not jump to conclusions. Let's go have a look. I'm sure you're wrong."

Abbi grabbed the sliding doors and pulled them open. She walked out, Meg coming up right behind her. Inside the house, all activity had ceased, as all eyes were on the two girls, who were walking out into the screened-in pool area. The bright sunlight glistened on the water, and the humid Florida air hit their faces and wrapped them like a blanket. Meg felt sick to her stomach as they approached the pool.

As they came closer, Abbi hesitated and stopped. Then she swallowed and looked up at Meg, who was taller than her.

"Wait. I think you might be... right. The hair... It can't be...."

Meg let out a resounding whimper as the realization sank into both of them.

"What do we do?" she squealed, bending forward and throwing out her arms. "What are we going to DO?"

"Okay, let me just think for a second," Abbi said. Her eyes fell on two guys that had stepped out on the back porch and were staring at the girl in the water.

"You two, come here and help me," she said. "We need to get her out of the water right now."

The two boys rushed to Abbi and took off their T-shirts, then jumped in. The tallest guy dove down and grabbed the girl's clothes, then pulled her toward the surface, where Abbi and the other guy held onto her, then pulled her up onto the deck. As they did, she rolled onto her back, and the hair slid from her face, so they could see who she was.

Bobby, the guy on the right, immediately recoiled when seeing her face. "What the…?"

The other guy, Trevor, screamed and let go of her shoulders. He pulled away, crabbing on his hands and feet to get away from her body.

"Wh…what?"

Abbi let out a shriek. They all three looked up at Meg, their eyes questioning.

"It's…" Abbi said, stuttering and barely able to find the words. "It's…."

"It's you," Trevor took over.

They stared at Meg like they expected her to have all the answers. Instead, she shook her head in disbelief, staring intensely at the girl's face.

"It's… me?"

Part I

FIVE HOURS LATER, COCOA BEACH, FLORIDA

Chapter 1

"WAIT. CAN YOU EXPLAIN THIS AGAIN?"

I looked at my sixteen-year-old daughter, sitting in front of me at the dining room table at our house. She had asked to talk, and I made hot chocolate for both of us, put whipped cream on top, then added a marshmallow to each cup. Olivia had rolled her eyes at me as I served it to her and told me I was making too big a deal out of it. I had told her that it was so rare these days that my daughters wanted to chat with me, so I felt it was appropriate and pulled out the bag of Oreos to go with it. Maybe I was just looking for an excuse to indulge a little since I had been dieting for two weeks and doing really well.

I felt we deserved it.

Olivia exhaled, annoyed. "What part didn't you understand?"

"Eh, all of it?"

"Mom!"

"Okay, so mostly the part where you say you don't have... a gender?"

"I do have a gender. I am just not a boy or a girl," she corrected me. "I identify as non-binary. Why is this so difficult?"

I threw out my arms. "I just don't understand it. Please, bear with me. Your mom is old."

"Like that's an excuse," she mumbled and sipped her hot cocoa.

"What's that supposed to mean?" I asked.

"It's just the same lame excuse that everyone from your generation uses when our generation brings up these things. 'We're from a different time.' That kind of stuff. But it's just a bad excuse for not wanting to learn."

I leaned back in my chair, slightly offended. "Okay? So now I can't ask you to explain it to me? I can't tell you that I don't understand how you can have no gender just because that's a bad excuse? I'm a little confused here, sweetie."

Olivia rolled her eyes and shook her head. "I just knew you would make this about you."

"Then don't explain it to me. Just let me tell you what I got out of this conversation so far," I said, leaning forward, tapping my fingers on the sides of my cup. "You're telling me that you're not a boy nor a girl; you're... no... bi...."

I made a strained face, and Olivia sighed deeply. "Non-binary, Mom. I've told you this a thousand times. It's called non-binary."

"Yes. Okay. So, that's what you are. And that means you have no gender; I got that right, didn't I?"

Olivia nodded. "Yes."

"And you want us to call you what?"

"My pronouns are they/them."

I wrinkled my forehead and tried my best not to seem insensitive. But the truth was that it was really hard for me to understand this. I wanted to since it seemed so important to my daughter, or rather... my...?

"So, what do I say when I introduce you to people? If I can't say, daughter or son? This is my...?"

"Child?"

I looked at her, barely blinking. "O-okay. And your name?"

"I want you to call me Ollie or just O. That's what my friends do."

That broke my heart. I had come up with the name Olivia when I was pregnant and had spent weeks convincing Chad that it was the right name. He had finally agreed, and I was so happy. To be honest, it was the name I was most fond of out of all my children's names. I simply loved that name. And now, I just had to let that go? Just call her something else. Or rather call *them* something else?

Oh, dear Lord, this is going to be hard. I am going to mess this up big time.

Ollie placed a hand on top of mine, then smiled. "You'll get it, Mom."

"I just thought that… well, when I saw you in that suit for your prom, I was so sure that you were just gay, or rather lesbian. I had never… I'm a little surprised; that's all."

"I know that I am mostly attracted to boys, but I have had a few girlfriends."

My eyes grew wide. "You have? How have I not known this?"

She shrugged and sipped her cocoa.

"I guess I just assumed the girls who came here were just your friends. I guess I haven't really paid enough attention, huh?"

She looked away, and that small gesture filled me with guilt. I hadn't been at home enough. I knew it, and now it was coming back to bite me. My kids needed my attention.

"Well, guess what?" I said, "I will pay better attention from now on and will make sure to get all those pronouns correct the best I can, okay?"

They looked up, and our eyes met. I saw relief in them, and I realized this conversation with me had taken a lot of courage on their part.

"Ollie," I said, tasting the name. "I could get used to that. It's kind of cute."

That made them smile, and I smiled back just as my phone vibrated in my pocket. I grabbed it and stared at the display, then realized it was Chief Annie from Cocoa Beach Police Department. I was about to take it when I realized Ollie's eyes were on me. Then I shook my head and put it back in my pocket.

"She'll just have to wait," I said. "I'm with my daug... my *child* now, paying attention to what *they* are saying."

"What if it's important?"

I leaned forward and grabbed my child's hand in mine, then caressed the top of it. "You're more important. Now, tell me more about how you found this out about yourself...."

As I was speaking, my cell stopped vibrating, but then my landline began to ring. I closed my eyes, annoyed.

"Someone really wants to get ahold of you," Ollie said.

"Just let it ring," I said, shaking my head. "So, how did you find out?"

"Well, I was on TikTok, and this person had made a video about being non-binary, and then I just saw that I recognized myself in the things that were being said, and then I...."

She paused when a police patrol car drove up our street and parked in our driveway. Someone stepped out and walked up to the house.

It was Matt—my ex.

"I guess it *is* serious," I said with a shrug.

Ollie stood to their feet. "I knew this would happen."

Matt knocked on the door. Ollie gave me a sad look, then walked toward the stairs. "Do what you gotta do."

"Olivia, please, what do you want me to...?"

She lifted her hand. "It's Ollie! Don't deadname me, please. And it's okay, Mom. Really."

But I knew it wasn't. She wanted my full attention. I cursed them all as I walked to the door and pulled it open.

"What do you want?"

Chapter 2

THEN:

"I'm pregnant."

Tom Hudson stopped chewing. His wife, Raina, looked at him anxiously.

"I'm sorry to just drop it on you like this," she added. "But I couldn't keep it to myself any longer."

Raina bit her lip, waiting for his answer. How was he going to react? Was he happy? She couldn't quite read his facial expression. His eyes seemed frozen almost, and his lips weren't moving.

Come on, for crying out loud. Say something!

Raina reached over and grabbed his hand, then smiled softly. "I mean, this is what we wanted, right? This is what both of us wanted?"

Tom was still frozen, but then something happened. His shoulders came down, his eyes eased up, and was that... a smile on his lips?

"That's... that's truly... amazing," he said.

Phew.

Raina sighed and let the relief rush over her. She didn't know why she had suddenly been so nervous to tell him. They had, after all, been trying to get pregnant for six months now, so there was no reason Tom wouldn't be happy. Maybe she was just worried that he had changed his mind?

She shook her head and felt happiness spread inside her. It didn't matter. She had misjudged him—misinterpreted his facial expression. It was all in her head. She always did this. She was always overthinking everything. It was exhausting. She had to start getting better at this type of stuff. It was going to drive them all nuts—especially now that the child was coming. There was so much to overthink.

"I'm so glad you feel that way," she said.

Tom laughed. "Wait. Did you think... that I wasn't happy?"

She shook her head. "No... no, I was just...."

Tom tilted his head and grabbed Raina's other hand in his. "Sweetie. I'm beyond excited. I thought you knew I wanted this baby as much as you do?"

She smiled and sighed softly. "I know you do. I know."

"Good," he said. "Now, we need to celebrate this. This is fantastic news. Waitress? Can we have the dessert card? This calls for a big piece of chocolate cake."

Raina laughed lightly. Tom always wanted to celebrate with chocolate cake. It was the same when they had bought the house and the sale finally came through. Then, he brought home a huge chocolate cake for them to share.

"I'm gonna be fat if we keep this up," she had said. "I almost hope we won't have a lot to celebrate in the future."

But tonight, they did have something to celebrate. Something huge.

"Let's have two pieces of the chocolate lava cake," Tom said and pointed at the menu.

"Of course, sir," the waitress said with a smile and left.

"This is so exciting." He grabbed her hands between his again. "Names. We need to think about names. When are you due?"

"In six months," she said.

"Oh, wow. Then we have a lot of work to do. We need to decorate the nursery. We need to get a changing table, a crib, the full Monty."

She sighed and looked into his eyes. "And we need to tell our families."

He paused, then looked away.

"Where is that waitress with our cake?"

"Tom, honey," she said and tried to get his attention. "Look at me."

He did, but she could tell it was hard for him.

"I know you don't have any contact with your parents, but don't you think now is the time to try and rebuild that connection? I want our child to have grandparents, and they deserve to know, even if you don't get along with them."

He pulled his hands out of hers.

"I'm sorry, honey, but that will never happen."

The chocolate cake landed on the table in front of them.

"Really?" she asked. "Don't you want them to know they will be grandparents?"

"Let's not talk more about this," he said. "Eat your cake."

"But...?"

He slammed his fist into the table, and Raina jumped. "Don't, just don't. I don't want you to mention this to me ever again. Do you hear me?"

Raina swallowed. Everyone in the restaurant was staring at them, and she lowered her gaze.

"O-of course. If that's how you want it."

"It is," he said with a small angry snort. Then he regained his composure. "Now, let's eat cake."

Chapter 3

"WHY DON'T you pick up your phone?"

Matt stormed past me into the house.

"We've been trying like crazy to get ahold of you."

"I'm sorry if I am not constantly available," I said and closed the door behind him. "But I was, in fact, having a very serious conversation with my oldest daughter, and now she is pissed at me. She needed me, Matt, so this better be important."

He ran a hand through his hair and sighed.

"It is."

I threw out my arms. "What is it then? Spit it out."

"They found a body. A young girl," he said. "Down in one of the rich houses in Snug Harbor. She was in the pool."

"Oh, dear," I said. "How old?"

"Nineteen or twenty. There was a party there last night—a bunch of college kids on spring break. One of the kids grew up in the house, and her mom was out of town. She invited a handful of her friends down for the week, had a party, and invited a bunch of her old friends from the area."

"I see, okay. That is serious and important. But why me?"

"I don't know. I haven't been down there yet. Chief Annie told me to get you as fast as possible."

"Now? I can't just... Angel is sleeping."

"Isn't Olivia home?" he asked. "She can look after her for a few hours, right?"

I exhaled. I had been using my oldest as a babysitter a lot lately. I would probably have to start paying her soon.

"Please?" Matt said, folding his hands.

"All right, I'll ask her," I said. "But it's Ollie now, in case you talk to her. She changed it."

He looked puzzled. "Ollie? Why?"

"It's a whole thing," I said. "Don't let me get started. Apparently, her pronouns are they and them instead of her and she. I've already messed it up several times, and I am sure I will again."

"Oh... wow," he said. "I will try and remember that."

I walked to the stairs, then turned to look at him. "Do you mind if Alexander Huxley tags along?"

He wrinkled his forehead. "That journalist? I didn't know he was here? Didn't he go back to Washington?"

"No, he chose to stay."

"But Eva Rae, we can't have a journalist snooping around a crime scene. Why would you even suggest that?"

"He's kind of... writing a book about me. He has asked to look over my shoulder while I work. He told me that I would be able to censor anything he writes, so he won't publish anything we don't want out to the public. We signed a contract on that and everything. He just wants to write about me."

Matt made a face.

"Really? Why?"

I paused. "You don't think I am interesting enough to write a book about?"

He looked flustered. "No, no, that's not why. I just... wondered why *he* wanted to so badly."

I sent him a glare. I couldn't let Matt know that I was into Alexander, and we had been on a few dates. It was too early to tell if it would become anything. I was definitely interested, but it could still go many ways at this point. I knew Matt would be hurt if he found out I was seeing someone. Matt had known me since preschool, and we had loved each other always and even had a child together. But the timing just wasn't right for us. We couldn't figure things out enough to stay together, even though the love was still there.

It was complicated.

"Well, I will have you know that he finds me very fascinating, or... at least my work, so that isn't that strange. Now, stay here while I talk to Olivia... OLLIE... sorry. Oh, boy. It's gonna take some time to get used to. Give me a minute."

Chapter 4

JUST KEEP BREATHING. *Just keep breathing.*

She realized she sounded a little like that confused fish in *Finding Nemo*, which her daughter used to love watching, but all she could do was repeat this in her mind. She needed to remain calm, no matter how much the world was on fire around her.

She had to answer all the questions slung at her and keep her head high, even though she was terrified.

Susan Kellam crossed her arms in front of her chest and looked down at her daughter, Meg, sitting on the couch. Her best friend, Abbi, was right next to her, holding her while she was crying helplessly. Young people were sitting everywhere, sobbing or staring blankly into the air. The police had asked them all to stay for questioning. There were at least twenty young people, most of them faces Susan didn't know. This was going to take all day.

"What on earth were you thinking?" Susan said with a light snort. "Having a party while I wasn't home."

"I... thought it would be okay," Meg said with a wail.

"I go away for one lousy weekend, and this is what I come home to? A destroyed house? A body in the pool?"

"I feel awful," Meg said. "I feel so terrible. It's so surreal; I can't even... I don't know how to...?"

"Yeah, well, you really did it this time, young lady. I can't believe you. I come home thinking I can spend the day with my daughter before she goes back to school. I even bought you a present and thought maybe we could go out for brunch or something. And what do I see when driving up the street? Police cars—ten of them, with blinking lights and everything, turning our nice neighborhood into a war zone. What will the neighbors say? And now they have completely taken over my house, walking around with their dirty shoes on my carpet. And don't think I don't see the way they look at me—like I am a bad mother whose daughter is completely out of control. Most of these kids here aren't even old enough to drink, Meg. *You* are not old enough to drink."

"I'm sorry," Meg said and hid her face between her hands. "I feel so terrible. It wasn't supposed to be this big. Just me and some friends, but then more showed up and soon...."

"And that's why you don't have a party," Susan snapped. "Because it gets out of control."

Silence filled the living room, where they were waiting for whatever would come next. Susan looked out the window at the activity by the pool. The body was still there, and the sight made her shiver. Someone was photographing it before it was put in a body bag. Susan felt how her breath got caught in the back of her throat.

"But... Mom...?"

Susan looked down at her daughter. Two officers walked past the living room, their radios scratching, their shoes leaving black marks on Susan's white carpet. She closed her eyes briefly.

Just keep breathing.

"Mom?"

"Yes, Meg? What is it?"

Meg swallowed hard. "W-who... who is she?"

"Who is who?"

She stared out the window. "The girl in the pool. Who is she?"

Susan made a face. "How am I supposed to know? I just got here and was told they had pulled a body out of the pool, then to wait here for questioning. Was she one of your little friends?"

Meg shook her head. "I don't know her."

"So, she was one of the uninvited guests, I guess. One of those that made sure things went out of control."

"But... Mom?"

Susan turned her head fast and glared at her daughter. Her daughter looked away, ashamed.

"What?" Susan asked.

Meg shook her head. "Nothing."

Susan exhaled deeply just as the door opened and someone walked in.

Chapter 5

"MAKE sure you stay in the back and don't get in the way. And please don't touch anything."

Matt looked at Alexander while narrowing his eyes. He wasn't even trying to hide that he didn't want him there, which was evident on the entire car ride there. Matt kept exhaling, annoyed, and shaking his head every time Alexander opened his mouth to speak. Even when he just asked me for a piece of gum, Matt shook his head with a *tsk-tsk*.

Alexander put up his hands and pulled back, resigned. Matt sent him a look to make sure he understood how serious he was and that he was the one in charge here. He was the man.

"Eva Rae!"

Chief Annie spotted me from where she was standing. She was talking to an officer who was showing her some paperwork.

"This has to wait," she said and put her hand on his shoulder. She used the other to wave at me.

"Eva Rae, so glad you're here."

She rushed to me and grabbed me in a firm hug. Chief Annie

was freakishly strong for a woman of her size, and her hug pushed out all the air from my lungs.

"How's the baby?" she asked when letting me go. "Matt says she's walking now?"

I tilted my head. "Well, not quite yet, but we're getting there."

I sent Matt a look, and he smiled, excusing himself. He liked to brag about our kid, I got that, but the fact was that Angel wasn't walking yet. She was still crawling and, every now and then, getting up on her feet by holding onto something.

It was his first baby. He had one other son, Elijah, but he didn't know him as a young child because the mom never told him he was a father. I forgave him for exaggerating.

"Oh, well, but I bet she's adorable still. You need to bring her down here soon, so we can all see how big she has gotten."

"What have you got for me?" I asked, trying to get to the point. "I hear it was a young girl in the pool?"

"Yes, come with me," Chief Annie said, and I followed her to the sliding glass doors leading to the pool area. It was crawling with techs in their body suits, and I put on a pair of plastic shoes and gloves. We walked to the poolside. It was so humid that I began to sweat almost immediately. Even for March, it was hotter than usual.

"Young woman, we think she's around nineteen maybe twenty years of age, was pulled out of the pool by young party-goers at eight twenty-five in the morning. Showed no sign of life, no pulse from the second they got her on dry ground," Annie said, walking so fast I could barely keep up with her. Her big golden belt buckle shone in the sunlight. She stopped at the body bag, then knelt next to it. She asked one of the forensics if it was okay, then opened it when he nodded.

My stomach turned when seeing the young girl's face come into the light. She was just a few years older than my Olivia... *Ollie, sorry.*

Her skin was pale and so delicate, almost seemingly paper-thin. Her blonde hair surrounded her face like a halo. The color had left her cheeks and lips, which told me she had been dead for quite some time. But it was always difficult with a body submerged in water to tell exactly when death occurred or even secure much evidence.

I looked at her chest and abdomen. "She's been stabbed several times; do we have the weapon?"

Annie shook her head. "We haven't found anything. At least not yet, but we will keep looking."

I exhaled and felt sadness creep over me. This girl was someone's daughter.

"So... who is she?"

Annie looked up at me.

"That's why we need you. We don't know who she is."

"But... I just walked past a girl in the living room who looked exactly like her?" I asked. "I assumed it was a sister, maybe even a twin?"

Annie stood to her feet and placed both hands at her sides. "That's what's so strange. They look exactly the same, yet the mother claims she only has one child. I already asked."

Chapter 6

"Wait a minute...."

They weren't the kind of words you'd want to come out of your doctor's mouth when doing your baby's first ultrasound, and immediately it had Raina's heart racing. Her mind became filled with all kinds of awful scenarios.

"W-what's wrong, Doctor?" she asked, clutching Tom's hand harder in hers.

"Give me a second to be certain," he said and stared at the small monitor.

Raina felt anxious. Tom tried to calm her down by caressing her hand. The gel on her stomach felt clammy and cold, and she couldn't stand the wait. What was going on? Why couldn't he just tell her? Was it so bad he couldn't say it to her face? Was the baby sick? Did it have too many fingers, or was it deformed in any way?

"Doctor Fabler?" Tom finally said. "Is something wrong with our baby? You're getting us kind of worried here."

"There it is... ah... no, wait, yes... there, see...?"

"What are we looking at?" Tom asked, worry in his voice. It was combined with a slight annoyance.

Raina struggled to breathe. Fear had gotten a grip on her. "Please, Doctor Fabler, what...?"

"Look," he said, interrupting her, then pointed. "It's right there. That little moving area right there. How amazing. How absolutely miraculously amazing."

"W...what is?"

"Right there," he said and pointed again.

Then he turned to look at her, and his mouth curved into a huge smile. "It's another heartbeat."

"Another heartbeat... but...?" she asked, looking confused at Tom. "Does that mean...?"

Doctor Fabler threw out his hands. "Twins. You're having twins."

Raina's breath got caught in her throat. She looked at Tom, worried about his reaction, then back at the doctor, her mouth open and eyes wide.

"Say that again?"

"Twins," he said. "It's so wonderful. I have twins at home. Two boys. They're a hoot. You have a lot to look forward to."

Raina swallowed. She looked at Tom. Twins? How were they supposed to handle two babies? One was okay, and she felt like she could do that, but two? How did that even work? How would she breastfeed if they were hungry at the same time? Would they wake each other up? Wouldn't it just be double the hassle? Tom worked so much; would she be able to take care of two children at once?

"That is so wonderful," Tom said and clutched her hand tighter. "I'm actually a twin myself. My mom always said that it was a handful at first, but the advantage came later because we always had one another, my sister and me. We were inseparable and would always play together...."

He paused like he realized he had said too much. Then, he went

28

quiet.

The doctor took over. "It is often genetical that if twins run in one family, then it's likely it will be passed on to the next generations."

The doctor wiped the gel off her stomach and printed the sonogram for them. Raina took it and thanked him before they left. Tom took her out for frozen yogurt after, and they sat in silence before she finally asked.

"You are a twin?"

His eyes avoided hers. "Yeah, well... let's not...."

"I didn't even know this. Why have you never told me?"

He shrugged and ate his yogurt with a small spoon. "I didn't think it was important."

"You didn't think it was important to tell me you have a twin sister?" Raina asked, surprised.

Tom scooped more yogurt on his spoon, and then it snapped.

"Now, look at that," he grumbled. "Why do they make these spoons so small? For crying out loud. Now, I have to go get a new one."

He rose to his feet and grabbed another spoon, then returned. "Can you believe how small these spoons are? Do they think only kids eat this?"

She gave him a look, and he paused.

"What?"

"I can't believe you have a sister, and you never told me."

"Yeah, well, it's not that important."

"We're starting a family here, Tom. I think it is important. Come to think of it, I know nothing about your background or your family. You never want to talk about them; why?"

He shook his head. "It's not worth talking about."

She ate from her strawberry yogurt with chocolate sprinkles. Tom didn't even look at her. It had been the same every time she asked him about his family since they met. He would either avoid answering completely or give her half sentences or sometimes get angry at her for even asking. What had gone wrong between them? Did that mean that their children would never know that part of their family? There could be cousins, aunts, uncles, and grandparents, and they'd never know them? Raina didn't even know if both his parents were still alive or if they were still married. Tom refused to answer every time she tried to turn the conversation in that direction. She had thought he'd come around at some point and hopefully start talking about it if she gave him time to trust her enough. But so far, it hadn't happened, and she was beginning to think it might never.

Was he going to avoid them forever? Didn't he want them to meet his children?

"It might change once he gets his own children," her mother had said when she discussed it with her and, if she was honest, complained about it. "A lot happens to a person once they have their own children."

Raina emptied her yogurt while staring at Tom, hoping her mother was right.

Maybe when the children are born. Perhaps then he will have a change of heart. Maybe he will soften up by then.

He reached over and grabbed her hand in his, then squeezed it. "I love you. You love me. That's all that matters right now. You, me, and the babies."

That made her smile.

"You're right," she said.

"I'm always right," he said with a sly smile. "Don't you forget that."

That made her laugh out loud. "Don't get too used to the idea. Soon, you will have to answer not only me but also two little ones. You're in for quite the ride, my friend. I hope you're ready for it."

He lifted her hand and kissed the top of it.

"It's all I want in the world. You and the babies are all I need."

Chapter 7

SUSAN KELLAM, who I had been told was the owner of the house, shot to her feet as I entered the living room through the sliding doors. Chief Annie was right behind me.

"Mrs. Kellam?"

She nodded.

I shook her hand. "Eva Rae Thomas, FBI. I have been asked to be a consultant on this case. Can we talk?"

She nodded again, visibly agitated. She pointed toward the couches. A couple of teenage girls were crying in the corner, hugging each other, while the rest just sat on the floor or the stairs, staring blankly into thin air.

"O-of course. Do you want to sit down?"

"Yes, that would be nice, thank you."

We all sat. Mrs. Kellam folded her hands neatly in her lap like I often had watched my mom do. It was usually a sign that she was nervous.

"S-so, who is she?" Mrs. Kellam asked and nodded toward the sliding doors. "The girl?"

"That's what we're trying to figure out, Mrs. Kellam," Chief Annie said.

I saw Matt in the corner of my eye. He was by the pool area, talking to a couple of colleagues. Alex was keeping his distance but stayed close to me.

"You don't know her?" I asked and glanced at the girl sitting next to Mrs. Kellam on the couch. She was the spitting image of the girl I had just seen lying in the body bag. It was almost creepy.

Mrs. Kellam looked at her daughter, then at us. "I... I have no idea who she is. I don't even think Meg knows, am I right?"

Her daughter shook her head. She was pale and looked like she could get sick at any minute. Mrs. Kellam shook her head in ragged movements.

"You'll have to excuse my daughter. She's... she was the one who pulled the... the body out of the pool. She's in shock."

"You haven't seen her?" I asked, puzzled. "The girl?"

"No. I came home to find the police here, and I wasn't allowed to go out there," Mrs. Kellam said.

I looked at Annie, who nodded. "We did ask her if she had any other daughters—if the girl could be her daughter, and she said no."

"It was a very strange question," Mrs. Kellam said.

"So, the girl isn't your child?"

"No, my child is here," Mrs. Kellam said and tapped her daughter's leg with a nervous laugh.

"But, Mom, I told you...."

"Okay, wait," I said, interrupting her. "But Meghan is adopted then, right?"

Mrs. Kellam looked appalled. "No! How could you possibly suggest such a thing? I gave birth to her myself nineteen years ago."

"And the girl out there isn't her sister?"

Mrs. Kellam shook her head. "Her... what? No. Why... I would... I don't understand. Why do you keep asking me that?"

"Could it be a cousin? Sometimes cousins are very similar," Annie said.

Mrs. Kellam shook her head. "Her dad was an only child, and my brother only has boys. I don't understand why you keep asking this?"

I exhaled. "Because... well, maybe you need to see for yourself." I nodded at Chief Annie. "I think it's time she sees it."

Chapter 8

"TIME THAT I SEE WHAT?"

Susan felt her heart rate go up drastically. What were they talking about? All these strange questions had her stirred up. Were they going to accuse her of something? It was, after all, not her fault that her daughter had a party while she was out of town, was it? Could they charge her with anything? They were underage and drinking, so maybe they could? But she couldn't have stopped it since she wasn't at home.

Maybe it was time for her to lawyer up? Just in case?

"Would you be so kind as to tell me what is going on here?" she asked, looking at the short, slightly stubby red-haired woman in front of her. This was getting tiresome. It was awful that they had a party without her permission, yes; that was beyond horrible, but why did she feel like they were treating her like a suspect? It wasn't Susan's fault that someone had fallen in the pool. She was probably drunk out of her mind.

"I need you to come with me," Eva Rae Thomas said and walked to the sliding doors. "Out to the pool area."

Susan exhaled. She had really hoped she wouldn't need to get

34

more involved in this. Was this really necessary? It wasn't enough that she had to live with the fact that someone had died in her pool? Every time she took a swim—which wasn't often anymore, but it did happen—she would have to be reminded that there had been a dead body in the water—a young girl. It was terrifying.

I will probably have to drain the water, right?

She followed the red-haired woman outside and was blinded by the scorching sunlight. Susan placed a hand to cover her eyes till they got used to the light and she could see. There were a ton of people walking around out there. Some were taking pictures, others dusting for fingerprints or taking shoe prints from the grass. Her backyard was a true mess, and it was going to be hard to get it back to its usual splendor after this—especially her Azalea bushes. Someone had trampled them completely. And the hibiscus that she loved so dearly looked awful! It was like a horror show out there.

Susan grimaced when someone in a blue bodysuit trampled through her marigolds. He picked up a piece of clothing from between them, put it in a plastic bag, and then carefully sealed it.

Susan closed her eyes briefly when seeing that it was a bra. She was going to have a serious talk with her daughter about this.

"Right over here, Mrs. Kellam," the police chief said and pointed at the black body bag on the pavement next to the pool's edge.

They stopped in front of it, and Susan felt a shiver go down her spine, despite the eighty degrees outside and the scorching sun lurking above their heads.

"Is this really necessary?"

Eva Rae Thomas placed a hand on her arm, then nodded. "I'm afraid so. We need to see if you know this girl."

"But I already told you I don't? If Meg doesn't know her, then how would I...?"

While she spoke, a man in a blue bodysuit pulled the zipper open, and the girls' face and torso came to light. Susan stopped talking and could barely breathe as the face appeared. She bent down to better see up close, then stared at the girl in front of her, barely able to breathe. The pool area started to spin, and she felt her heart race so fast it hurt her chest.

"Do you recognize this girl?" Eva Rae Thomas asked.

"But that's imposs..." Susan paused, then looked at her daughter standing in the opening to the living room. She looked down at the girl in the bag, then back up at Meg.

"But... but I don't... I don't understand? How... how is this...?"

"I want you to think this through, Mrs. Kellam," Eva Rae Thomas said. "And try to remain calm and focused. Do you know who this girl is?"

"Yes, that's my... that's my daughter. That's Meg."

She glared at the girl in the bag, her heart pounding in her chest. There was a loud whooshing sound in her ears, and she could tell that people around her were speaking to her, but she could no longer hear them.

She didn't feel the spinning ground hit her either as she slammed her face into the pavement.

Chapter 9

"SHE'S GOING TO PASS OUT!"

I ran to grab Mrs. Kellam, but I wasn't fast enough. She deflated almost like a punctured balloon and fell to the concrete below before any of us could catch her. I knelt next to her. I reached down and touched her head, then placed it in my lap. My fingers came back covered in blood.

"She's hurt."

"I'll call for an ambulance," Annie said and grabbed her radio, then walked away while speaking into it.

"Mrs. Kellam?" I asked, trying to wake her. "Susan?"

I felt her throat and got a weak pulse.

"Susan?"

"Mom?"

Meg had come out to us and knelt next to Susan.

"She just passed out," I said to calm her. I could see the panic painted on her face.

"But... the... blood?" Meg said, her voice shivering.

"She hit her head when she fell," I said. "She'll need some stitches."

Susan groaned and blinked her eyes. Meg leaned in over her.

"M-Mom?"

"Meg?"

Susan tried to sit up but got dizzy and laid back down in my lap.

"Rest," I said. "We need to get you to the hospital."

"What happened?" she asked.

"You passed out."

She remembered. She gasped for breath and felt her head. "Meg. Oh, dear God. Meg!"

She tried to sit up again, but I pulled her back down. "Please. You need to wait for the ambulance to get here."

"But... Meg... my daughter... the girl in the bag, that's my daughter."

"No," I said. "Your daughter is sitting here next to you."

Meg grabbed her mother's hand in hers. "Mom, I'm right here. I'm here."

Susan stared at her daughter, blinking and narrowing her eyes. Then I felt her relax again.

"But... I don't understand," she said. "How is this possible?"

Annie came back out and signaled me.

"The ambulance is here," I said, relieved.

Susan's head was bleeding heavily, and had soaked my jeans. I was getting worried for her. I turned my head to see the EMTs come through the backyard with a stretcher. They attended to her briefly, then lifted her on the stretcher and rushed her away. Meg went with them, looking terrified as she got into the back, and they closed the door.

"Poor kid," Alex said as he came up behind me.

I nodded, thinking of my oldest kid, who was only a few years younger.

"Yeah, it's been a day," I said.

"You okay?" he asked, placing a hand on my shoulder.

I smiled, looking up at him, when I spotted Matt out of the corner of my eye. He was staring at us, and the look in his eyes made my heart drop. He was hurt.

I pulled away from Alex, then walked past him with a brief, "I should get back."

Chapter 10

THEN:

She was getting heavy. Raina could almost see the difference for each day that passed when looking in the mirror. She would stand naked in front of it in the bathroom, then turn to the side and feel her growing stomach. It seemed almost impossible that it could get any bigger than this, but her doctor said it would.

"You have to remember that you're carrying not just one but *two* babies."

Oh, there was no way she was forgetting that. All night long, when they fought inside her and kicked and moved, she was reminded that there were actually two of them. And Raina—if she was being honest—was a little terrified at having to deal with two babies instead of just one like all of her friends. Her best friend, Emma, had recently given birth to a baby boy, and she had vividly told Raina how much work such a little creature demanded. And Raina had seen it for herself when visiting her friend and seeing the messy house, along with her friend's exhausted eyes. And Emma only had *one* baby.

Raina was going to have two? It seemed impossible.

It'll be okay. Others have done this before you. You can do it.

Raina got herself dressed, even though it was getting harder to do so by herself, then walked to the store to get some fresh strawberries. She had been craving those since the beginning of the pregnancy, and today, for some reason, more than ever. She walked in, wearing her big loose maternity dress and a coat thrown casually over it since she wasn't cold these days. It could snow and rain and blow the coldest winds, but she was always warm. It was her big belly that kept her warm, her mother kept telling her.

"It's like walking around with your own heater strapped to you," she would laugh.

Raina failed to see what was so funny about that. She was so hot at night too, and now that spring was coming, and everything was warming up, it was only getting worse.

Raina opened the fridge and grabbed a couple of cartons of milk, enjoying the cold air from inside of it as it hit her face.

She leaned on the glass as she closed it again, feeling dizzy. The doctor had told her that her blood pressure was very low due to the pregnancy, and she had to be careful when getting up or turning suddenly. He explained that the blood would take a while to get to her head.

"Are you okay?"

An elderly man had approached her. He looked concerned.

"Do you need any help?"

Raina smiled and let go of the glass. "I'm okay. Just a little dizzy."

Even though she smiled reassuringly, he still looked concerned, and she started walking to the produce area to get those strawberries. She would eat them with milk and sugar on top, something her grandmother had always served her as a child, telling her it was a Scandinavian tradition. Right now, even the thought was like heaven to Raina. She couldn't wait to get home and eat. It was like it was all she could think about these days.

As she went toward the produce area, a woman passed her in the cereal aisle. Their eyes met, and the woman smiled gently, then looked down at her stomach. Something about her, something in her eyes, made Raina stop.

"Excuse me," she said as she passed Raina, and Raina stared at her, even long after she had walked past her. She didn't know why. There was just something about this woman that she couldn't quite put her finger on.

It was like she knew her.

Oh, dear Lord, the pregnancy hormones are messing with you, Raina.

Raina chuckled at herself, then grabbed the strawberries and walked to the check-out. While putting her groceries up, she kept looking behind her, as she felt like someone was watching her. When she paid and was about to leave, she spotted the woman in the long beige trench coat standing in one of the lines. Their eyes met again, and a shiver of cold ran down Raina's spine.

Then she rushed outside, closing her coat as she walked home, wondering who that woman was and why she was staring so intensely at her.

Part II

THREE DAYS LATER

Chapter 11

"THIS ISN'T RIGHT."

I rose to my feet and walked to the whiteboard. We were having a meeting in the war room we had put up at the newly built Cocoa Beach Police Station that had just been finished a few months earlier. The rooms were much bigger than the old station and the workplaces quite nice. I was glad to see my old colleagues move out of that old building across the street, where they had been since the sixties. The building had been damaged during Hurricane Irma, and it rained inside sometimes, causing mold to grow. It was about time they got some nicer work conditions.

"I can't believe we can't figure out who this girl is?" I said and looked at her picture on the board in front of me. "Isn't anyone missing her?"

We had spent the morning going through all the facts, what we knew and what we didn't. We knew that the cause of death was stabbing. The girl had five stab wounds in her stomach, chest, and abdomen. The autopsy concluded it killed her before she hit the water. And then she probably fell into the water, where the killer left her. They had found traces of her blood on the area around the pool, but it was sprayed in a fashion that was consistent with multiple stabbings being done rapidly after one another, pulling out the knife and reentering it. The knife hadn't been found yet. The time of death was determined to be around seven a.m. that same morning. The body had sunk to the bottom due to water filling the lungs.

All this we knew. All this was straightforward information.

What we still didn't know was who the heck this girl was.

"We're still waiting for the DNA-test results," Matt said. "Hopefully, they'll tell us who she is."

Our eyes met, and I felt sadness overwhelm me. We had a huge argument the day before when he dropped off Angel after having her for two days. He had told me he wasn't comfortable with Alexander being around his daughter so much, so if I would please make sure to only see him when our child wasn't there.

I completely lost it. Not because of Alex, but because Matt had introduced Angel to one girl he dated after the other. I had wanted to tell him to stop so many times but kept quiet because I didn't want to argue with him. And now he started this? Just because Alex had been there when he picked her up. We had just been talking about the case and the day at the house, how seeing the girl had made me feel, and so on for the book. It wasn't even romantic, even if Alex had held my hand just as Matt walked in, of course, without knocking first, like he always did. Because it had never been an issue before, but now it was. And apparently, that made Matt angry, seeing us sitting there, sharing a moment of intimacy. I argued that Angel was napping and hadn't been around Alex at all, but Matt wouldn't let it go.

It drained me. I hated this. I hated how hard it was for us both to move on, how painful it still was to be around one another. I hated how hurt he got, and I loathed how hurt I always felt when seeing him with someone else. How long was it going to take us to move on? Because we couldn't be together. It was simply not doable. Believe me, we had tried.

Why did he still hold so much power over me?

"And none of the kids we have spoken to knows her or has seen her before. When seeing the picture of her, they all say, *but that's Meg*," Matt added with a shrug.

"They do look identical," I said, looking at Alex, who had gotten permission to observe the meetings and my work, but only if Chief Annie got to approve the chapters where this case was mentioned.

"But that means the mother must be lying," Chief Annie said. "I have gotten the birth records from Cape Canaveral hospital where Meg was born nineteen years ago, and according to them, Susan Kellam only gave birth to one child on December 8th of that year. It makes no sense."

"Someone is lying," I said. "And someone killed this poor girl, someone very angry with her. Let's meet again when we have more news. I want to make a profile of this killer and a possible motive, but it's really hard to figure out why someone wanted to kill her when no one knows who she is."

Chapter 12

"I'M BEING DISCHARGED LATER TODAY."

Susan was so happy to say the words to her best friend, Tina. She had called her up as soon as the doctor had finished his morning rounds and told her she was finally going home. She had been so excited she had gotten herself dressed even though there were hours until she would get to leave.

"I can't believe they kept me for three days."

"Well, you did have a fractured skull," Tina said. "It can be quite serious."

"It was a minor fracture," Susan said.

"Better to be safe than sorry," Tina said. "I, for one, am glad they ran those last tests to make sure there was no bleeding in the brain."

Susan nodded. Her friend was right. And staying at the hospital for three days had given Susan time to think. It was a necessary break and rest that she much needed, even though her brain kept circling the same subject.

The girl in the pool.

Susan kept seeing her face in front of her eyes, and she couldn't stop sobbing every time.

"Are you going to be okay?" Tina asked. "I can pick you up and make sure you're settled into the house. I can fill the fridge and check on you in the morning. I can also stay the night if you want me to?"

"No, that won't be necessary. But thanks for offering. Meg is here. She will pick me up later."

"When is she going back to college?" Tina asked.

"She called them and said I was in the hospital, so they gave her an extra week before she needs to return."

"Okay, that's good. So she can keep an eye on you until you get better. I worry about you, sweetie. I don't like this one bit. The girl they pulled out of your pool. How awful. You must feel terrible. Are you sure you want to stay at that house again after what happened?"

"I'm sure," Susan said. "You know how much I love my house."

"But still...." Tina trailed off. "The entire backyard is blocked off, and all that police tape, constantly reminding you of...."

"I know. It's unpleasant. I will have to see what it's like. Or I might take you up on your offer."

"Please do. Nothing would bring me more joy than having you here. I can't stand thinking of you in that house where that poor girl was murdered."

Susan went quiet. Her head was starting to hurt again. Maybe it was just talking to Tina that made her exhausted. She was always so dramatic. Susan closed the conversation, hung up, and then placed the phone on the table. She closed her eyes briefly, feeling very tired. She had been feeling this a lot these past days—like she could barely keep awake.

Soon, she dozed off and had the oddest dream about Meg when she was a little girl. She woke up, gasping for air, just in time to see someone standing at the foot of her bed. Susan clasped her chest, catching her breath when his face came into sight.

Then, she screamed.

Chapter 13

I WASN'T GOING HOME. Of course, I wasn't. I wasn't going to just sit on my hands either. Instead, I decided to go to the hospital. I knew Susan Kellam was still admitted there, and I wanted to have a quick chat with her. I just wanted to do it alone, without Alex or Matt there with me to cloud my judgment.

There was something this woman wasn't telling me. There had to be. And I was getting tired of it.

Someone is lying here, and I need to figure out who.

I thought that maybe if I got her to myself, then perhaps she could tell me the truth. It was only a matter of time before we got the DNA results, and then we would know.

I just didn't have the patience to wait for it.

As I parked the car in the parking lot, my phone rang. I picked it up, and to my luck, it was the medical examiner, Elena Mendez.

"I thought you would want to know this right away," she said. "You told me to contact you directly."

"Yes?" I turned the car off and sat back. The hospital front entrance was constantly flocked by people coming in and out of the sliding doors. I felt oddly excited. "What do you have for me?"

"Your Jane Doe shares her DNA almost one hundred percent with the first sample you gave me," she said.

"With Meg Kellam?"

"Yes."

"So what does that mean? What can we make of that?"

"That they are, in fact, siblings and twins."

I smiled. "Identical twins?"

"Yes."

"So, she is nineteen like Meg. But we can't determine her exact age from DNA, right?"

"No, we can know a lot from DNA but not the age. You will have to get an analysis of the biomarkers, maybe from her teeth or bone growth. That's not my department."

"All right, and the other sample?"

"That's a match."

"It's a match? So, she is the mother? Susan Kellam is the birth mother of both of them?"

"Yes."

"I'll be… well, thank you so much. Send over all the paperwork, okay?"

"Will do."

I hung up and stared at my phone. I had a feeling Susan Kellam was lying, and I was right. But I just couldn't understand why. And why did the hospital records state that she only gave birth to one child? It made no sense to me. Something was off here, and the questions were piling up.

I grabbed my purse and put my phone inside it, then exited the car and walked up toward the entrance, thinking it was about time Susan Kellam started answering those questions.

Chapter 14

"YOU! W-WHAT ARE YOU DOING HERE?"

Susan jumped up in the bed, staring at the man in front of her. He smiled, almost smirked. The very sight of him made her heart drop. Tears sprang to her eyes as the realization sank in.

Oh, dear God!

"Y-you."

"Yes, me."

"It was you."

"It sure is," he said, nodding.

Susan sank. "But... but... why?"

"You know why."

"I don't understand...."

"Don't act so surprised. You knew this day would come."

Susan jumped to her feet, pushed him aside, then stormed out into the hallway. She could hear him laughing still as she stormed down the hallway and hurried into an elevator. She pressed the buttons frantically, and as the doors started to close, a hand was placed between them, stopping them from closing. Susan pushed the buttons again, trying to get them to close, but the doors slid open, and in stepped the man who had been by her bedside.

"Do you think you can run away from me?"

He pushed the buttons, and the doors closed. That was when she spotted the knife hiding halfway up his sleeve. Susan pulled away, her back against the wall. Sweat was springing to her forehead as fear and panic rushed through her.

"What do you want from me?" she asked, her heart thumping in her chest. The elevator moved downwards, and Susan looked at the numbers as they passed the floors, hoping it would stop at one of them, readying herself to scream for help if it did.

The man smiled and placed the knife on her throat. Susan couldn't breathe. She stared at the numbers as they went down: third floor, second, then first.

The elevator stopped and dinged. The doors slid to the sides. People appeared who were waiting for the elevator. Susan opened her mouth, intending to scream, to alert the crowd, when the man whispered in her ear.

"This was your lucky break. But don't stop looking over your shoulder from now on because I will hunt you down."

Then the knife was swiftly removed, leaving a superficial cut on her skin, and the man exited the elevator just as a flock of nurses and doctors entered, all wrapped up in their own worlds and chatting away happily. Susan stood with her back against the wall as the elevator doors closed. She was still gasping for air as it began to move again. She stayed inside the elevator for several minutes, going back up, then back down before she dared to exit into the lobby. She stormed toward the sliding doors and out into the parking lot.

As she went through the doors, she spotted the red-haired FBI agent who walked inside just at that exact second. Susan turned her face to the side so she wouldn't be recognized, then slid away, covered by a crowd of busy, rushing people.

Chapter 15

I HATED the smell of hospitals. I absolutely loathed it. I don't know why. Maybe because it always reminded me of bad things happening. Today was no different. The smell hit my face as I entered the lobby and asked for Susan Kellam's room. It lingered in my nostrils still as I was in the elevator and got out on the third floor.

I walked to the room and peeked inside behind the curtain.

The bed was empty.

"Susan?"

"Can I help you?" A nurse came up behind me. I showed her my badge. She looked flustered at the sight. "I'm looking for Susan Kellam?"

"She's not there?" the nurse asked and looked behind me. "That's odd. She was there half an hour ago when I was in there with her pills. She is being discharged later today, but not until three o'clock."

"Could she have gone to the bathroom?" I asked.

We both looked at the door to the restroom next to us. It was left ajar. The nurse peeked inside, then shook her head.

"She's not there either."

I glared at her bed and then at the table. "It looks like her phone is still here. And her purse."

"She must be here somewhere then, right?" the nurse said. "I mean, she can't just have left without her stuff?"

I stared at the empty bed and Susan's things while the nurse alerted a security guard and her colleagues. I didn't like this. Something was very much off. Unease was spreading throughout my body. I grabbed my phone and called Chief Annie.

"Susan Kellam has run."

"The mom? Really?"

"Yes, I went to see her in the hospital, but she left, and her phone and purse are still here. I think she knew I was coming; maybe she spotted me from the window and made a run for it."

"But why? Why would she run?"

I bit the inside of my cheek. "I'm not sure. But she is definitely lying to us. I just got the results from the lab, and she *is* the mother of our Jane Doe in the pool. Maybe she realized that I had figured her out, and that's why she ran when seeing me arrive?"

Annie went quiet for a few seconds. "Okay, I will ask all patrols to be on the lookout for her. She's a person of interest."

I hung up, a nagging worry in the pit of my stomach.

Why is Susan Kellam running from us? What is she hiding?

The nurse came back, shaking her head in distress. "They can't find her anywhere."

I handed her my card. "Call me if Susan Kellam shows up, please. Or if you have any news about her."

"O-of course."

"Thank you."

I smiled at her, then rushed to the elevators and pressed the button while wondering, if I was Susan Kellam, where would I go to hide from the police?

Chapter 16

THEN:

She had a cesarian, and the twins arrived one Tuesday afternoon while it was still snowing outside the windows. IAnd just like that, Raina was a mother of two. Most people at the hospital and those who visited couldn't tell the two of them apart, but to Raina, they were like night and day. Where one, Charlotte, was so gentle and easy and slept most of the time with a blissful smile, the other, Noah, wouldn't stop crying and constantly demanded to be fed and would scream endlessly if the milk didn't run fast enough, stressing Raina out.

She stayed four days at the hospital while trying to figure out breastfeeding. It was harder than she had expected, and there was constantly one that needed to be fed, leaving no breaks for Raina.

She was feeling so drained—like they literally sucked all the life out of her. Well, it was mostly Noah who was making things hard. Charlotte was so sweet and gentle; it was sometimes like they almost forgot about her because Noah demanded so much attention.

Yet Raina loved them both with all her heart, and as soon as they came into her life, she couldn't imagine being without them. And when they were taken from her to sleep with the other babies, she would sneak down and peek at them through the glass window.

On the third day, when the babies were napping in the afternoon, she went down and stared at her babies, her eyes filling with tears of gratitude. To think that she could be so lucky to have those two creatures in her life. It was almost too hard to believe.

She was about to turn back and leave when someone entered the room from the other side and stood by the window. Raina paused for a few seconds. She stared at the woman in the beige coat who had come in before she remembered where she had seen her before.

It's the woman from the supermarket. The one who kept staring at you. Why is she here? Why is she looking at your children?

"Do I know you?"

The woman didn't turn to look at her, and Raina couldn't see her face properly, but she recognized her anyway. Raina stepped forward.

"Excuse me?"

She didn't answer, nor did she look at Raina.

Raina cleared her throat to get the woman's attention, then tried again.

"Excuse me? Who are you here to see?"

The woman didn't turn to look at her; she just stood there, staring at Raina's babies. It freaked her out.

"Excuse me, do you know any of the babies here?"

When she still didn't answer, Raina stepped closer and reached out her hand to try and touch her shoulder, to get her to turn around. But instead, the woman pulled away and rushed toward the door.

"Hello? Excuse me?" Raina yelled after her. "What are you doing here?"

The woman was gone. Raina stood for a few minutes, her hands shaking heavily.

Then she rushed after her and alerted a security guard on the way. They searched for the woman for hours afterward, but she was nowhere to be found.

That was when Raina decided never to take her eyes off her children again.

Chapter 17

MULTIPLE CARS WERE BLOCKING the driveway, so I had to park in the street. I walked up and knocked on the door. It was Meg's close friend Abbi who opened the door.

"Hi, Abbi, Eva Rae Thomas, FBI."

"I remember you," she said.

"Can I come in? Is Meg here?"

She nodded and let me inside.

"She's in the kitchen."

I followed Abbi into the kitchen, where Meg was sitting at the round table with four of her friends, all faces I recognized from the party. They were drinking Starbucks coffee.

"Hi, Meg," I said. "Can I talk to you for a second?"

She nodded and put down her cup. One of the guys, Trevor, who I had a feeling was her boyfriend, placed a hand on her shoulder for comfort.

"What's up?" Meg asked as I pulled her aside.

"I'm looking for your mom," I said.

"She's at the hospital. I'm going to pick her up at three."

"Except she isn't," I said. "I came straight from there, and she wasn't there. She left her belongings, though. Her phone and purse were still there."

Meg looked up at me, eyes worried. "You're telling me she's missing? Did something happen to her?"

I looked at the girl in front of me, wondering how I was going to tell her that the girl in the pool was her sister. She deserved to know.

"I... We don't know what happened. But I came looking for her here. I thought she might have come home."

"Well, I haven't seen her," she said. "I've been with my friends."

"I see that. She hasn't tried to contact you or anything?" I asked.

Meg shook her head. "I was supposed to pick her up later today."

"Okay."

"Wait, do you think she might be in danger?" Meg asked, her voice cracking.

"What's going on; are you okay, Meg?" Abbi asked from the other end of the kitchen. She put her cup down and approached us.

"Mom is missing," Meg said, touching her hair.

Abbi's eyes grew wide. "What?"

"We don't know if she is missing," I said, trying to calm them down. "There might be a perfectly natural explanation."

Trevor rose to his feet. "Are you okay? Meg?"

Meg hid her face between her hands. "I just... I can't take anymore. Where could she be?"

Trevor walked up to her and put his arm around her shoulder.

"Does your mom have any friends?" I asked. "Anyone she might go to?"

Meg looked at me, then shrugged. "I... I'm not sure."

"What about Tina Walsh?" Abbi said. "Meredith's mom. Aren't they still friends?"

"I think so," Meg said. "I mean they... they had a falling out last year, and I haven't been home much so...."

I nodded and wrote down the name. "Okay, I'll try and look there. And then there is the tricky question of your father."

Meg's eyes grew big and wide. "What about him?"

"I know he hasn't been in the picture during your childhood, but we would like to talk to him anyway. Do you know where we can find him?"

She shook her head. "No, I don't. I never knew him."

"Did your mom ever talk about him?"

"No."

"So, you don't know how to contact him? Do you know his name?"

"No. She never mentioned him."

"Okay. I will try and find him some other way then."

I paused, knowing I had to tell her. The right time to tell someone this type of thing wasn't going to come. She saw it in my eyes.

"She was my sister, right? The girl?"

I exhaled, then nodded. "Yes. I'm afraid so."

"Don't be. I kind of guessed that she was," Meg said. "I just... well, I feel awful for never having known her. And now, I never will. I always felt like something was missing in my life—like I had a sister somewhere. I had this strange feeling, like a hunch. Guess that's just a twin's sixth sense, huh?"

"I guess so," I said. "Again, I'm sorry to be the bearer of such bad news."

Chapter 18

MEG WATCHED the FBI agent through the window. She observed her as she got into her car and took off. Trevor came up behind her and kissed her neck.

"Stop," she said. "I'm not in the mood right now. Didn't you hear? My mom is missing."

He stopped kissing her but kept hugging her from behind. "They'll find her. Don't worry."

She pulled out of his grip with a deep groan. "I'm just scared that something happened to her. My mom doesn't just disappear like that. And I'm scared the police won't be able to find her. I don't trust them. I think they're all useless."

Trevor threw out his arms with a smile. "How about we start a search of our own, huh?"

"What do you mean?"

"We got cars. We don't just have to sit here and wait. I say we drive around town and look for her."

Meg looked into his eyes, then nodded. "Take action ourselves. I like that very much."

Trevor smiled. Abbi and Bobby came into the living room.

"What's going on?" Abbi asked.

"We're gonna go look for Mrs. Kellam ourselves. In our cars," Trevor said.

"We can help," Bobby said.

"Great. You and Abbi can go in your car," Trevor said. "Then Meg and I will take my truck."

Meg grabbed her phone and wallet, then followed Trevor into the driveway, where his blue Raptor was parked. He held the door for her, and she crawled in. A hunting knife was on the seat between them, and Trevor took it, then placed it in the glove compartment before starting the truck.

He backed out of her driveway and took off down the street.

"Gosh, that Bobby annoys me," he said, almost spitting as they reached the end of the street and he stopped.

"Why?"

"It's nothing," Trevor said and took a right.

"Apparently not," Meg said.

"All right," he said and turned onto A1A toward downtown. "You should have heard him when you were talking to that FBI agent. He kept going on and on about who he thought killed that girl at your house."

Meg stared out the window, then narrowed her eyes. "And who does he think it is?"

"It doesn't matter," Trevor said and passed a garbage truck. "You know how people talk."

"No, tell me. I want to know. What are they saying?" Meg asked.

Trevor laughed. "It's silly, really, but Bobby seems to think your mom might have killed her. He thinks that's why she ran off."

Meg chuckled but didn't really find it funny. "Yeah, that's crazy."

"Mrs. Kellam killing someone. That's one for the books," he said, still laughing.

Meg didn't answer as she stared out the window.

"Wait, you're not telling me you actually think your mom could kill someone?"

Meg shrugged. "What am I supposed to think? I didn't think she would lie to me all my life either about having a twin sister. I feel like I barely know her anymore. Maybe I never did."

"You can't be serious," he said. "It's your mom."

"Why hide my sister from me my entire life? How will she explain it? Why wouldn't she kill her if she suddenly showed up?"

"That's crazy talk," he said, but he was no longer laughing, and the grin was gone from his lips. "Let's just find her, okay? I'm sure there's a logical explanation for all of this. There has to be."

Meg exhaled and looked out the window. "I sure hope you're right. I sure hope so."

Chapter 19

IT TURNED out that Tina Walsh lived only two blocks south of Susan Kellam's house. I called Matt at the station and had him find the address, then text it to me, and minutes later, I was driving onto her street and parked in front of her house. I knocked on the door, then waited.

A woman opened it.

"Yes?"

I showed her my badge. "Tina Walsh?"

She looked terrified. "Y-yes? That's me. Can I help you?"

"Can I come in?"

"Yes, o-of course."

She stepped aside, and I walked in. The house was decorated in light blue and green colors and beachy designs, as many of the homes in Cocoa Beach were. The mirror in the hallway was in a frame covered with seashells, and on the door hung a wooden sign saying GONE SURFING.

"How can I help?" Tina Walsh asked.

"I'm looking for Susan Kellam."

"Susan? But... she's in the hospital; I know because I talked to her this morning. She is being discharged now, actually. Or in a few minutes, that is."

"I went there earlier, and she wasn't there," I said. "She left behind her phone and purse."

"Oh, really? That's strange."

"That's what I thought, too," I said. "I need to talk with her, so if you see her, please let me know."

"I haven't. I haven't seen her in a long time, actually. I've only spoken to her on the phone. It's awful what happened. I can hardly believe it. That poor girl. Do we know how she died?"

I nodded. "We're working on the details."

"Yes, yes, of course, you can't reveal that to me. But do you know who did it? They said in the news that she had been stabbed?"

"We're still working on that part. But I really need to...."

A young woman entered the living room where we were standing.

"Meredith," Tina Walsh said. "This is my daughter. She's the same age as Meg and the others."

"But you weren't at the party? I don't recognize you from the list of witnesses?" I asked.

She shook her head. "No. I don't hang out with them. "

"Meredith doesn't like to party the way the others do," Tina explained.

"Mom," Meredith said.

"It's the truth, isn't it?"

Meredith shook her head, annoyed like my own children always did to me. "I need to borrow the car."

"The car? Well, okay. Where are you going?"

"Just downtown," she said.

"Okay," Tina said and gave her a set of car keys.

"What's going on here?" she asked and nodded in my direction.

"The police are looking for Susan," Tina said. "She's gone missing, and we're worried something has happened to her."

"Mrs. Kellam? Really? I just heard someone saw her behind Publix."

I stared at her. "Where did you hear that?"

"Someone wrote it in the group chat. Look." She pulled out her phone and showed me a text.

OMG I JUST SAW MEG'S MOM SITTING BEHIND PUBLIX LOOKING LIKE A HOBO

I read it, then looked at Meredith. "Thank you so much. You've been a great help."

Chapter 20

SUSAN WAITED a few minutes before walking into the living room. Tina was still standing there, looking out the window at the car that was driving away. Then she turned to face her.

"Do you think I pulled it off?"

"I hope so," Susan said.

"Do you think she could hear it in my voice that I was lying? It was shaking badly. Heck, my entire body was trembling. I was so scared. I'm a terrible liar—always have been."

Susan nodded. "I appreciate it. I hope you know this."

Tina hugged Susan. "Anything for you."

They let go of one another, and Susan looked at Tina's daughter, who was standing next to them.

"Thank you, Meredith. Your part was brilliant."

Meredith laughed. "It's not that hard to send yourself a text."

"But it certainly worked excellently," Tina said. "She couldn't get out of here fast enough."

"But calling me a hobo?" Susan said with a grin. "That was a little strong, don't you think?"

That made them all laugh.

"Whatever it takes, "Susan continued. "Thank you, kid."

"You've always been good to me," Meredith said. "Even though your daughter doesn't like me much."

"You've always been like a daughter to me," Susan said and hugged her.

"All right, let's get you out of here," Tina said. "Before this FBI woman realizes she has been tricked and comes back."

"Where will you go?" Meredith asked.

"I'm taking her out to the beach house," Tina said. "I canceled this week's renters and paid them back their money. She can stay there."

Susan hugged Meredith again.

"Take care of yourself," she said as Susan followed Tina to the garage and got into her SUV. They backed out of the driveway and drove down the street.

The beach house was located by Sixth Street. Susan had been there a few times when Tina and her husband Carl held summer parties there. It was a five-bedroom house and way too much space for her, but it would serve as a good hiding place. It was usually rented out through Airbnb, and no one would suspect Susan being there.

"I can't thank you enough," Susan said and hugged her friend as they arrived at the house and walked inside. "I can pay you to make up for the missing rent."

"Nonsense," Tina said. "Don't worry about it."

"You're a really good friend. I hope you know that."

They hugged again.

"Anytime, sweetie. Just stay safe, okay?"

"And you're not even going to ask me why the police are looking for me?"

"You'll tell me when you're ready," Tina said and pecked her on the cheek. "I trust you."

Susan watched her friend leave and waved at her, wondering how long she could keep fooling everyone. It made her sad to do this to her best friend—having her lie to everyone, even her husband.

But it was the only way out.

Chapter 21

"HOW STUPID DO you think I am?"

I mumbled the words, sitting inside my car as I watched Tina Walsh leave the beach house on Sixth Street. I had waited on a side street until they drove past me, then followed them there.

They thought they had me fooled, but I could tell that the text Meredith showed me had been sent by herself. It was her own profile picture at the top of it. But I decided to play along—to lure Susan out of hiding.

"I found her," I said as I called Chief Annie. "She's staying at a house on the beach."

"Good," Annie said. "Do you want to bring her in for further questioning? As a person of interest?"

I watched as the garage door closed to the yellow beach house. "Not yet. Now that I know she is safe, I will need more ammunition before we let her know we're onto her. She won't tell me anything the way it is now anyway. I don't have enough. I caught her in one lie, but there might be more."

"Has she tried to get in contact with her daughter?"

"I don't think so. The daughter seemed sincerely surprised that she was missing—and concerned too."

"Do you think she killed her? The mom?"

"I don't know. I fail to see why."

"She obviously tried to hide her existence for nineteen years," Annie said. "Maybe her showing up made her fear she would be revealed."

I nodded pensively to myself. "But she's still her mother."

"Moms kill too," Annie said. "I have seen it more than once."

"True. I just wonder where this girl has been for nineteen years. We still don't even know her name. How far are we on tracking down the father? She might have been living with him."

"There's no name on Meg's birth certificate," Annie said. "It's harder said than done."

"We need to find him. Somehow," I said. "Did you run the DNA from the girls in the system? Maybe find a match there? If he is in the system?"

"Yeah, that's our best bet right now," Annie said. "I'll contact the lab."

I looked at my watch and realized it was getting late. "I need to get home to my kids. My mom has to leave. She has a date."

"Is Elizabeth still seeing that same guy?"

"Irvin? Yes. They're like teenagers. It's a little disturbing, to be honest."

That made Annie laugh. "Good luck with that."

"Thanks."

I hung up, then took off down A1A toward Minutemen Causeway and took a turn. Before going toward my house, I passed Fat Donkey and the Tiny Turtle, two of my favorite places to eat and get ice cream. I stopped for the red light in the intersection when I spotted a blue Ford Raptor. Inside it, I saw Meg and Trevor as they drove past me. I wondered about them and if I should call her and let her know that her mom was okay. I wasn't sure I believed her when she said she didn't know who her father was. Something in the way she reacted made me doubt she was telling me the truth. People always thought it was so easy to lie to the police, but I had learned to decode the small details over the years. A nervous tick, a slightly vibrating lip, or the way they spoke, like if they repeated the question that had just been asked, or simply irregular speech. Any change in facial expressions or speech patterns could indicate that they were trying to get away with a lie. Sometimes, they said too much, sometimes too little. Sometimes, they redirected their eyes or fidgeted excessively. There was a lot to look for. But one thing I knew was that if I suspected someone was lying, I was usually right.

The question was, how did I get Meg to tell me who her father was?

As the light turned green and it was my turn to go, I knew exactly how I was going to pull that off.

Chapter 22

"I'm telling you, this woman was staring at our children. It was creepy."

Raina looked at her friend, Anne, who had come to see the babies. They had been home for three weeks, and things were getting better. The twins still demanded Raina a lot, especially Noah, who seemed to be constantly hungry or needy in some way.

"That sounds scary," Anne said and sipped her coffee.

"Are you telling that stupid story again?" Tom said as he walked into the kitchen, putting down his briefcase.

"You're home early," Raina said as he kissed her cheek.

"Yeah, my five o'clock meeting was canceled," he said, looking through the mail on the counter.

Raina shook her head. "Tom doesn't like me telling the story of the woman. He thinks I'm being paranoid."

"You *are* being paranoid," he said. "Why would some old woman look at your children?"

"To steal them, hello?" Raina said. "Have you not heard of trafficking? They steal children and sell them as sex slaves and what-not. Twins are in high demand, I have heard. There are freaks out there who will pay a lot of money to have sex with identical twins. That's what I read. Or maybe they can sell them to families who can't have children. That happens too."

That made Tom laugh. "You've got to be kidding me. Don't believe everything you read. I'm sure she was just a nice old lady vising her grandchild."

He walked out, and Raina shook her head. "He can say what he wants. I am not letting the babies out of my sight."

She glanced at the baby monitor, where she could watch her babies napping on the screen. They were right upstairs in the nursery, but still, she didn't take any chances.

"I told you that it was the same woman I saw at the supermarket too, right?"

Anne nodded and sipped her coffee. She took a cookie from the plate that Raina had put out and ate it. Raina knew how crazy she sounded, but she also knew what she had seen. If she was being paranoid, it only served as a precaution. There were so many creepy people out there—lunatics and crazy folks. You never knew what could happen to your poor child or children.

"I am telling you, this woman wants my babies," she continued.

Anne looked at her watch, then rose to her feet. "I... it's late... I should go."

"Oh, okay?" Raina said. She was sad that she was leaving already. It was so rare these days that she got to talk to another adult human being, let alone a woman. She missed seeing her friends. Babies were wonderful, but they were also a lot and didn't exactly make great conversationalists. "But you've only been here for twenty minutes?"

"I have to be somewhere; besides, you need your rest," Anne said and kissed her cheek.

"Let me walk you out," Raina said and followed her to the door.

Anne grabbed her coat from the hanger and put it on, along with her boots. Then she smiled awkwardly.

"Please, get some rest, Raina," she said. "You seem... a little out of it."

"Oh, really? I guess I am tired. Having twins is exhausting."

Anne grimaced. "You really need to take better care of yourself."

She turned around and walked down the steps of their town-home toward her car, which was parked in the street. As she opened the gate to the fence, Raina raised her hand to wave. At that moment, she spotted someone standing across the street from her house, on the sidewalk.

It was her.

"It's... it's... HEY!" Raina started to yell, and Anne turned to look at her.

"What's that?"

Raina walked down a step. "It's that... it's that... woman again..." she said and pointed.

The woman in the long coat realized she had been seen, turned around, and started to walk away. Anne looked concerned at Raina.

"That's just an old woman going for a walk."

"But... but... it's... her again... she was staring at our house. She was just standing there, watching us."

Anne tilted her head. "Please, go take a nap, will you? Let Tom take the babies for a little while. You're overworked."

"But...?"

"Just do it, okay? And call me tomorrow. I'm worried about you."

Chapter 23

ALEXANDER WAS SITTING on my porch when I got back home. I stepped out of the car and walked up to him. He looked disappointed.

"I had a feeling you ditched me," he said.

I smiled awkwardly. "I'm sorry. I had some stuff to do."

He rose to his feet and approached me. "How am I supposed to write a book about you when you don't let me be a part of your most important work?"

"It wasn't my most important work. I wouldn't say that. I was just following a hunch," I said.

He sighed and placed his hands on my shoulders. I felt like a child being caught doing something bad.

"I need to be a part of everything you do," he said. "Every little tiny detail could turn out to be important. I need to be a part of the entire story here."

"I understand that," I said. "This was just something I had to do alone."

I unlocked the door and entered the house, Alexander following me. My mom was in the kitchen, cooking, and it smelled awful. I wasn't much into my mom's health food, but I guess it was good for my children and hopefully for my weight as well in the long run.

It just didn't taste very good. At least, I didn't think so. But my two oldest children had come to love it, so that was good, I guess. As long as they didn't demand that I cook it once my mom left.

"Finally," my mom exclaimed and pointed at her watch. "You know I have plans tonight."

I spotted Angel sitting in her high chair, eating pasta with her fingers. I leaned down and kissed her.

"I know, Mom. I came home as fast as I could."

She wiped her hands on a towel, then looked at me with that glare that made me feel five years old again.

"Well, it wasn't fast enough. Now, I'm late for my date."

She said a brief hello to Alexander, then rushed out the door, grabbing her purse on the way.

"Say hi to Irvin," I yelled after her, but I don't think she heard me. It didn't matter. I grabbed my daughter, pulled her out of the chair, and held her in my arms. Gosh, how I loved coming home to that smile. It was priceless—the best thing in the world. I was making funny noises while talking to her when I realized Alexander was watching me and taking notes.

"Is that gonna be in your book too?" I asked and put my baby down so she could crawl to her toys and play.

"You're darn right it will. This is the other side of you, the one no one knows or gets to see," he said. "The caring mother. They're going to love it."

That made me chuckle. "Are they going to be reading about the mess in my house too?"

That made him laugh. "Probably. It shows you're human."

"You're crazy," I said.

"I'm crazy about you," he said.

I was picking up pasta noodles from the floor when he said it. I paused and stood up straight.

"What?"

He smiled. "You heard me. The more I get to know about you, the more I like you. I'm nuts about you, Eva Rae. I think I'm falling for you."

That left me speechless. I mean, I knew he was interested, and we had kissed a few times and been on a couple of dates, but I didn't know he was actually that into me. I didn't understand why. He was such a handsome guy, and he could have any woman. Why me? I was just plain Jane. As I stared at him, not knowing what to say, how to reply, I wondered if I was crazy about him too. I wasn't sure. I liked him, yes. But I was still too attached to Matt and still getting over that breakup. Maybe I just wasn't ready to fall for anyone?

"It's okay," he said. "You don't have to say it back. It's not like I said *I love you*."

"Mom?" my oldest had stepped inside the kitchen and came to my rescue.

"Olivia!"

I said it way too loud and didn't realize my mistake until it was too late, and she sent me a glare that could kill.

"Ollie, sorry! I will get it right someday. I'm sorry!"

Ollie grumbled loudly, then left the kitchen, slamming the door behind her. No, let me correct that—behind *them*.

Boy, this was hard.

Chapter 24

IT WAS SO peaceful at the beach house. Susan sat outside on the patio until long after the sun had set behind the house. She loved sitting there, listening to the waves crash on the shore, the big Atlantic Ocean kissing the coast. It had always been her favorite sound.

She had opened a bottle of wine that she found in the kitchen, in the cabinet that they kept locked from the renters. She was certain that Tina wouldn't mind. She could always pay her back later. Susan needed a glass of wine—or two or three—more than anything in this world. She had a lot to think over and decisions she needed to make. Her heart was aching deeply, and she worried about how this would end. As she closed her eyes, she kept seeing her child's face, lying there lifeless on the ground by the pool. She knew it was her child; of course, she did.

She just didn't understand how it was possible.

"Where did you come from so suddenly?" she asked into the darkness. "And why did you come?"

Susan understood why the police would want to talk to her. She understood that very well. She just couldn't risk her secret being revealed. It was too unbearable—too much for her. For so many years, she had forgotten all about it, trying to forgive herself for what she did, what she had to do.

And now it had all caught up to her.

It really was true what they said. You couldn't just run from your past. Yet she had believed she could. She had truly believed she could just start over and never look back.

"What a fool you are," she told herself while sipping more wine. It was a really nice red, probably one Tina had saved for later, or maybe it was even Carl's. He was the one who liked red wines, whereas Tina was a white wine girl, just like Susan usually was.

Just not today. Today, it didn't matter what she drank, to be honest, as long as it served to calm her nerves.

"What am I going to do?" she cried out after the fourth glass, and the bottle was almost empty. "How am I going to move on from this?"

She drank the rest directly from the bottle and felt the wine's effect on her body. She stayed in her seat but soon dozed off in the chair. When she woke up, the bottle was on the ground, shattered, and she realized she had pushed it in her sleep. She reached down to gather the pieces of glass but cut her finger and started to bleed.

"Shoot," she said and looked at the blood dripping onto the ground. She pushed herself up from the chair and staggered toward the sliding doors, blood running down her hand. She walked through the doors and found a tissue, then wiped it. It wasn't deep, luckily, and soon it stopped bleeding. Susan sighed, then decided it was time for bed. She was about to walk outside to bring the cushions inside in case it rained when a noise made her turn and look toward the hallway. In the doorway to the kitchen, she spotted a figure, a shadow.

"W-who is there?"

The man stepped forward into the light. Susan gasped.

"I told you I would hunt you down," he said.

Susan saw the knife in his hand and panicked. She staggered back and fell to the tiles.

"P-please."

The man shook his head. The knife was lifted and aim taken.

Part III
TWO DAYS LATER

Chapter 25

MEG SIPPED her Starbucks cold brew that Trevor had gotten for her. He had been staying with her for the past few days while her mom was missing. The same night that they had been out looking for Meg's mom, Tina Walsh had come to the house and told Meg not to worry.

"Your mom is safe. I just thought you should know."

Trevor had told her he would stay with her until her mom came home so that she wouldn't be alone through all this. He would sleep on the couch, he said. But of course, he had crawled into Meg's bed several times at night, trying to get some action. But Meg hadn't wanted to. She had kicked him and told him to leave her alone. For some reason, that made him try even harder and want her even more. Meg didn't understand why that was.

"I can make us some eggs? Do you want eggs?" he yelled from the kitchen.

"I'm not hungry," Meg yelled back. She was staring out the window of the sliding doors leading to the pool. She could still see the girl in the water; the images wouldn't leave her brain, no matter how hard she tried to force them out. They were lodged in there forever.

"You still thinking about that body?" Trevor asked as he came into the living room and saw her. She sipped her coffee and nodded.

"It's hard not to. She had my exact face. It was so creepy."

Meg shivered as she said the words. She could still remember the feeling it left her with when seeing the face. It was hard to shake.

"It was really creepy," he said and hugged her from behind. "Made me sick to my stomach, to be honest."

He said the words, but Meg didn't think it sounded like he meant them at all. There were no emotions behind them. She suspected that he found this whole situation a little exciting as well. He seemed so fascinated with it and the body and kept talking about it all the time.

Like he found it mesmerizing.

"Yeah, well, I just wish they knew who killed her," Meg said and pulled out of his hug. "I hate that there's a killer here somewhere and that he was here at the house, at the party."

"Kind of like the *Scream* movies, huh?" Trevor said, sounding a little too enthusiastic for Meg's taste. She knew he loved those movies and had watched the latest one that came out recently five times.

"Except this is real life. And the girl in the pool was my sister. A sister I could have known and been with my entire life if my mom hadn't lied to me."

He bobbed his head. "Yeah, you're right. You gotta be bummed out about that."

"I'm not just bummed out," she said. "My entire world has crumbled. Can you imagine that? I don't even know who to trust anymore."

He grabbed her by the shoulders. "Hey, you can definitely trust me, okay?"

She nodded and calmed down. "Of course. I just... I can't stop thinking about how my life could have been different had I known I had a sister."

"You have often told me that you dreamt that you had a twin," he said. "How you felt like a piece of you was missing."

She turned away and faced the windows again. A bird was pecking at the tree outside when she spotted a car drive up in her driveway.

"Oh, shoot. It's her again."

"Who?"

"The FBI-woman. I wonder what she wants now."

Chapter 26

SHE OPENED the door before I could even knock. Meg stared at me, eyes fiery.

"I don't want to talk to you," she said before I could tell her why I was there. "Unless you have found out who killed my sister? Or where she has been for the past nineteen years?"

I cleared my throat. She had surprised me when opening the door so swiftly. I wasn't prepared for that. I had told Alexander to wait in the car as I didn't want him to mess up my plan. He wasn't too satisfied with that, but I told him this was as close as he would get.

"We haven't, but...."

"Then I'm not interested," she said and tried to close the door on me. I put my foot in it to block it.

"Hear me out, please."

She rolled her eyes at me. "Make it fast."

"You in a hurry? You got somewhere to be?"

She smiled mockingly. "What's it to you?"

"I thought you might like to know that we have a suspect in the case, and we're bringing him in later today. I have sent people to bring him in."

Meg's eyes grew wide. "Really? Who is it?"

"We have reason to believe your biological father is involved in the murder of your sister. That's all I can say as of right now."

She almost dropped her jaw. "My father? Really?"

I nodded, studying her face closely. "Yes, we have enough on him to bring him in and question him as a suspect."

She wrinkled her forehead. "But... but why would he kill her?"

"That remains classified. I just wanted to give you an update."

She looked pensive. "You know who my dad is and where he is?"

I nodded. "Yes. I'm sorry that you have to learn this way. I wish it were through better circumstances."

She scoffed. "Yeah, me too."

I stared at her, scrutinizing her face and her every move. I listened to the sound of her voice—it had changed, just a little, but enough for me to notice.

"All right, then. I will keep you updated. Any news from your mother?"

She looked up at me, eyes big. "N-no. Nothing."

I nodded. She was lying, but I already knew that. "She hasn't tried to call you or contact you in any other way?"

"No."

"Okay. You know where to find me if she does," I said.

"Yes."

I turned around and walked back to the car, then got inside. Meg slammed the door shut behind me, and Alexander gave me a look.

"Exactly what it is you expect her to do next?"

"Contact her father," I said. "If she does, in fact, know where he is or how to reach him, my theory is that she will try to warn him. To tell him that we're coming for him."

"And just how will we know if she does contact him? Do you have her cellphone bugged or something?"

I smiled, started the car back up, and then drove into the street. "It's way simpler than that. A girl like Meg is smart. She's not gonna risk anything by using her own cell phone to call him, but this house has a landline. I have asked the phone company to get me the records for the next twenty-four hours."

"Clever," Alex said with a grin.

"Well, it's not exactly airtight," I said. "I'm just praying that she will do what I think she will. If she doesn't, then we're getting nothing."

Chapter 27

THEN:

Raina was breastfeeding while it was pouring down outside her window. She liked the sound of the rain tapping on her roof while Noah ate greedily from her breast. It was the third time this night that he was hungry, and she had to feed him, while Charlotte slept peacefully in the crib as usual and rarely demanded to be fed at night anymore. At six months, the babies were getting big and heavy, especially Noah, who seemed to be growing faster than his sister.

Raina felt exhausted and leaned her head back in the rocking chair. The sound of the rain pouring down outside felt soothing, and she dozed off a few times, only waking up when her head fell forward and a pain shot through her neck.

"Are you done soon, little buddy?" she whispered, hoping he would let go so she could put him down.

But Noah kept eating, and there was nothing else to do except wait for him to feel full enough to stop.

He slowed down, and Raina stared at him, hopeful that she could finally return to her warm and cozy bed. She only hoped that

Tom wasn't snoring because that would simply be too much for her.

I'll kick him out of the bedroom if he as much as grunts.

Raina couldn't remember ever feeling this tired in her life. It was like there was no room for her just to breathe. And she could forget about eating. She couldn't remember when she had last sat down and enjoyed a proper meal. She always had to just grab something on the go before the next diaper change, feeding session, or naptime. For some reason, the two of them rarely managed to sleep at the same time, so there was always someone whose needs she had to tend to.

"Are you done?"

Raina looked down at Noah, feeling how he seemed to be dozing off. She felt relief, but just as she relaxed, he woke up again and latched back on like he hadn't eaten in days.

"This is never going to end," she mumbled as she leaned her head back once again and briefly closed her eyes. She dozed off again, and when she woke up, Noah was done and had finally let go completely. He was sleeping on her arm, looking so innocent and cute that she immediately forgave him for being so needy all the time. How could she stay mad at that face?

She rose gently, careful not to wake him, then walked to the door and out into the hallway. She always breastfed in the little office because she didn't want to wake up Charlotte in the nursery. There was always that risk she had to be careful of, that they woke each other up. There was nothing worse than both of them crying at the same time. She hadn't really figured out how to breastfeed two at a time yet. She knew it was possible, and some twin moms did it, but somehow, she hadn't mastered it.

"Now, we'll just get you back to bed, and mommy will get some much-needed sleep," she whispered as she approached the nursery.

She was only a few steps into the hallway when she noticed a light turned on inside the nursery.

"What the...?"

Raina rushed toward the door, thinking it might have been Tom getting up to get Charlotte. Maybe she woke up, and Raina had somehow not heard her?

"Honey?" she put her hand on the door and pushed it fully open, then almost dropped baby Noah from her arms.

A woman stood inside the nursery, looking down at Charlotte, who was still sleeping in the crib.

It wasn't just any woman. It was the woman from the hospital and the supermarket.

"What are you doing here?" Raina said angrily. "You have no right to... How did you get in? Why are you...? What do you want...?"

The woman turned around and looked at her. The look in her eyes made Raina stop talking.

Chapter 28

SHE WATCHED the FBI-woman leave in her minivan, then turned around and walked out of the living room.

"What are you doing, Meg?" Trevor asked, following right behind her. "Where are you going?"

She continued up the stairs and hurried into her mom's bedroom. She walked to her dresser's top drawer, pulled it open, then searched through it. She closed it, then opened another drawer and searched through that one as well. When she didn't find what she was looking for, she went to the nightstand and opened the drawers one after another until finally, she took out a small black book.

"What is that, Meg?" Trevor asked and came closer.

Meg put the book on the bed and opened it. Then, she smiled.

"Is that your mom's address book?" he asked. "Why do you need that?"

Trevor sat down on the edge of the bed next to her. "What exactly are you looking for?"

Meg turned a page and stopped. There was an old postcard

lodged in between the next two pages. She took it out and turned it.

"Bingo."

Trevor looked at the picture, then at the words on the back.

"Is that your...?"

"That's from my dad, yes. It says so here in the letter. Look, my grandmother sent it. She wrote that my dad sent it to her house, and she even told my mom to contact him so he would stop calling my grandmother and asking for her whereabouts. And both his number and address are on the back."

"What are you going to do with that?" he asked. "Will you give it to the FBI woman? Why didn't you tell her you had it?"

Meg looked up at Trevor, then smiled. "I don't want her to know. I need to warn him that he is a suspect."

Trevor gave her a strange look. "But...why? You haven't had any contact with him for your entire life?"

She shook her head. "I don't know. I just feel like it's something I have to do, you know? I really don't think he killed my sister."

Trevor shrugged and leaned on his elbow on the bed. "Why not? You don't know him at all."

She exhaled. "I know. I just...."

She didn't listen to him anymore but went to the phone next to her mother's bedside and picked up the handset. It was an old-fashioned wireless phone with push buttons in the handset, just like you would often see in old movies from the nineties.

She dialed the number on the postcard.

"What are you going to say to him?" he asked. "You can't just call him up after all this time?"

Meg stared at him while clutching the phone so hard that her knuckles turned white. There was a tone.

"It's ringing," she said.

"Are you sure you've thought this through?" Trevor said

nervously. "I mean, what if he really is the killer? If he murdered your sister, maybe he wants to kill you too? I don't think you realize what you're getting yourself into."

The phone kept ringing.

"Think about it," Trevor continued. "There's a reason why the police are looking into him. You might become an accomplice or something. You might get yourself in a lot of trouble."

Another ring. Then a crackling sound, followed by a stern voice. "Hello?"

Meg stared at Trevor, eyes wide. She couldn't say anything. No words would leave her throat.

"Hello?" the male voice said again. "Who is this?"

Their eyes met, and Meg didn't know what to do. Trevor seemed terrified.

"Hello? Is anyone there? Hello?"

Meg could barely breathe. She stared at Trevor, then leaned over and hung up.

Chapter 29

IT WAS ALMOST TOO EASY. I got the phone records for the past twenty-four hours in an email from the telephone company the next day, and as I went back to the time around when I visited Meg, there was a number that someone had called just a few minutes after I left the house. No one else seemed to be using the landline within that time frame, so this one really stood out.

I looked it up and realized it was a Canadian number. Through Canada411, I found the address. It led me to a small town called Mont Tremblant, north of Montreal in the Quebec Province.

I stared at the number and address on my screen, then wondered if it could really be him. Could that be the dad?

Chief Annie came up behind me, coffee in her hand. She handed me the cup. "Thought you might need it."

I smiled and looked up at her. "Thanks."

"What are we looking at?"

"I think I might have found the address for the dad, but I'm not one hundred percent certain."

"Maybe try and call him? Ask him?" Annie said, sipping her own coffee.

I held mine between my hands while thinking. "That's what I thought. But I really feel like this isn't something I should do over the phone. I mean, I need to be able to look at his face when I ask him what happened with his children. It's too easy to lie over the phone. On the other hand, it might not be him at all, and even if it is, maybe he won't even talk to me, so I'd risk going up there for nothing."

Chief Annie nodded pensively. "What do your instincts tell you?"

I looked up at her, then smiled. "That I should be on a plane already."

"Then that's what you need to do. I will call the local police in Montreal and tell them you're coming. I have worked with them before. We have a good relationship. A few years ago, we helped them catch a serial rapist who had come down here thinking he could hide in Cocoa Beach. They owe me one."

"That's settled then," I said. "I just need to call my mom and have her take the kids; then I will get my fat ass on a plane up to the cold."

"I envy you," she said. "It's getting hot and muggy here already, and spring has barely begun. It was eighty-six yesterday in my backyard. Can you believe it?"

I chuckled and finished my coffee. "Oh, I believe it."

I put my cup down, then thought about Alex. I had promised he would be able to follow my work for the book. I was going to need to let him tag along with me. I didn't mind too terribly since I really enjoyed his company for the most part. I just didn't want him to get in my way. If this guy had something to hide, then I really needed to be able to look into his eyes when I interviewed him and not have anything or anyone disturb me, no matter how handsome he was.

I grabbed my phone and called him to let him know.

"I'm ready whenever you are," he said.

. . .

Chief Annie left me, and I walked to Matt's desk, then sat on the edge. He looked up at me, lifting his eyebrows.

"You want something, don't you?"

I smiled. "Can you take Angel for a few days? I'm going to Canada, and my mom will take the big kids, but she doesn't really do well with the young one."

He scoffed. "Of course."

"Okay, great. Thanks."

I got up and started to walk away when he stopped me. "Wait. Is that Alex guy going with you?"

I turned around and smiled awkwardly.

"Don't tell me he is. Oh, Christ. Are you two dating or something?"

I made a face. "Dating? No, where did you get that from?"

"Then why is he going with you?"

"He's writing a book, remember?"

Matt scoffed again. "As if. He just wants to get busy with you."

That made me laugh. "Get busy with me? What does that even mean?"

"You know what it means."

I shook my head. "You're acting like a jealous boyfriend, and it's frankly getting a little old."

I turned around and left, feeling a pinch in the pit of my stomach, wondering why I always let Matt get to me the way he did.

Chapter 30

THEN:

"Who are you? And what are you doing in my house?"

Raina could barely breathe, and the words came out unevenly. She was so angry she wanted to scream at this woman. Who did she think she was? Just walking into people's houses? And what was she doing there? Stealing Charlotte?

The woman approached her. She was shorter than Raina and didn't look very strong, but you never knew. She still thought she could take her if she needed to.

The old eyes looked softly at her, and Raina eased up slightly.

"I... I'm not here to... I'm here to talk to you," she said.

"And so you come here in the middle of the night?" Raina asked. "Who does that?"

"I have been trying to talk to you for a long time."

Raina's shoulders came down. She looked at Noah, who was luckily still asleep and not disturbed by these strange circumstances.

"It still doesn't really explain why you're here in the middle of the night," Raina said. She walked to the empty crib and put Noah inside it carefully so she didn't wake him.

She walked back to the woman who grabbed her arm, then squeezed it hard. "What are you doing?"

"I've come to warn you. I couldn't come during the day because I'm afraid of your husband seeing me."

Raina wrinkled her forehead. "Tom? Why? How do you know my husband?"

The old woman let go of her arm. It was still hurting where she had clutched her skin.

"He is my son."

Raina stared at the small woman, then swallowed. "Excuse me?"

The woman nodded. "Yes. I am his mother."

"I... I don't understand," Raina said.

"Tom wouldn't want me to come," the woman said. "If he knew I was here, he would kick me out."

"Listen, this is all... it's very late, and I'm very tired...."

"No! You must listen to me. You must protect your children."

Raina felt confused and a little angry, to be honest. "Protect my children? What do you mean?"

The old woman's eyes grew worried. She shook her head. "Your husband, my son, is a murderer."

"A murderer? What on earth are you talking about?" Raina asked.

"He killed his sister many years ago when they were both still children. She was his twin. He strangled her. They were playing in the treehouse, and I was in the kitchen when it happened. At first, I thought they were just having fun, but then I realized— too late —what was really happening. Tom had his hands around her neck and squeezed all the life out of her. I dropped the pot with the stew I had in my hands and ran out there. By the time I made it to the treehouse and got his hands off her, it was too late. She wasn't breathing. When the police asked what happened, I told them I did it. I took the blame and served twenty years in jail to protect him. I realize now that I should never have done that. I'm afraid he's going to harm the children or you, my dear. That is why I have come, and that is why I have been following you. I wanted to keep an eye on you and the children and warn you against him."

Barely had she finished the sentence before the door opened to the nursery, and Tom rushed inside, holding a baseball bat in his hand.

"M-mom? Raina?" His eyes grew angry, and he spoke with a loud voice, looking from one to the other. "What on earth is going on here?"

Chapter 31

WE LANDED in Montreal the next day around five o'clock. Alex slept most of the way in the airplane, while I almost threw up because of all the turbulence. I was scared half to death while this guy just slept. I didn't understand how it was possible. Even the flight attendants had trouble and couldn't serve us anything to eat or drink for the three hours the ride lasted.

"How could you sleep through that?" I asked when we took down our carry-on luggage from the overhead bin.

Alex smiled and looked at me with his annoyingly well-rested eyes. "Oh, I can sleep through anything. I used to be a war correspondent, and I learned to sleep through the sound of bombs falling nearby and sirens going off. This was nothing compared to that."

"All right," I said and dragged my carry-on after me as we left the plane. I was still shaking from holding onto the armrest so tight, thinking I was going to die. But apparently, this was nothing. *Could've fooled me.*

We walked through the airport, and I showed my badge to the man behind the glass, along with my ID. Alex showed them his press credentials. The guy let us through, and we found a cab and had him take us to the Montreal Police Station, where Chief Annie told us to go. The air was already cold on our faces, and when coming from Florida's burning heat, you couldn't do anything but enjoy that sensation.

"Agent Thomas?" the guy asked with a heavy French accent after I had said who I was in the reception and she had called for someone. He stretched out his hand. I shook it. "I'm Detective Adams. I'm supposed to make you feel welcome, so... welcome."

That was a little odd to me. He didn't seem like he in any way wanted to be there or to have to talk to us.

"Thank you?" I said.

"I have a desk for you in here. It's over there," he said and pointed at an empty desk in the farthest corner of the station. "Let me know if you need anything, okay?"

"Okay," I said and looked at the desk. It wasn't much of a workstation, really. There wasn't even a chair. I turned to ask him if he had one, but as I did, I realized he was already long gone. And he hadn't exactly told me where I could find him in case I actually *did* need something. I guessed he didn't really mean it when he said it. I looked around, then saw two empty chairs leaning against a wall and grabbed them. I put them down for Alex and me to sit on, then pulled out my computer and logged on.

"Mont Tremblant is a small ski area about two hours' drive from here," I said. "It looks like this guy lives right downtown."

"When do you want to go up there?" Alex asked.

"It's late now," I said. "We'll go in the morning. I'll borrow a car from here, and then we can drive there ourselves. I don't want any of these snooty detectives tagging along and putting their noses in our business."

Alex wrote on his pad.

"Don't put that in your book, please."

He chuckled. "Why not? I like that you're so good at taking matters into your own hands. Shows your strength."

"Okay, but could you maybe remove the word snooty? It doesn't make me sound very nice."

"I'll have to see about that," he said with a grin. "What's in it for me?"

I lifted both my eyebrows. "You get to write a book about me. How's that?"

"Yeah, well, I was more thinking in the line of dinner once we have checked in at the hotel."

I exhaled, then smiled. "Okay. But snooty is out then."

He nodded. "Snooty is out."

Chapter 32

DR. MILTON SAT in the kitchen with his laptop on the table in front of him. Molly and Karl were playing on the floor behind him, screaming his ears off. Milton closed his eyes briefly and pinched the bridge of his nose.

"Be quiet, you two," he yelled. "I'm trying to work here."

"But, Da-a-ad," Karl said. "Molly is taking my doll."

"It's my doll," Molly said.

"No, it's not."

"It so is."

Karl pulled the doll out of Molly's hands, and Molly let out a wailing sound. Dr. Milton turned around and looked down at them. They both went quiet immediately.

"Don't make me get the belt," he said.

Two sets of big brown eyes stared back up at him.

"N-no, Dad. We'll be quiet," Karl said.

"And give me that darn doll," Dr. Milton said and pulled it out from between Karl's hands. The boy almost burst into tears but held it back, knowing the consequences if he didn't.

Dr. Milton snorted and looked at the doll, then placed it on the table in front of him. "Real boys don't play with dolls anyway, Karl."

His wife, Ashley, appeared in the doorway. She had a concerned look on her face. She was so young that she still had patience with the children and never approved of him getting upset with them over little things.

"Come, kids, let's go to the park and give Daddy some time to work."

Both kids rose to their feet and rushed to their mom. She helped them put on their coats, gloves, and beanies, and soon, Dr. Milton heard the sound of the door slamming shut behind them. He exhaled, relieved. Having children was her idea, not his. He felt he was too old, but she had begged him, so he had finally accepted it. But on the one condition that she took care of them. Dr. Milton wasn't a man who cared much for children; his passion and devotion belonged to his research work. If she wanted those little stink bombs around, then it was her job to make sure they didn't get in the way of his work.

"Ah, peace and quiet, finally," he said as he watched them outside the window. They walked down the street, holding their mother's hands.

Satisfied, he rose to his feet, then walked to the kitchen and poured himself another cup of coffee. He looked at the mountains in the distance, where he could see the slopes and the skiers zigzagging downhill. He was hoping to get a little action in himself this weekend when he was done with his article. But at the rate he was going, with all the silly and unnecessary interruptions, he probably wouldn't be done until sometime next week.

Dr. Milton slurped his coffee, then walked back to his laptop and sat down in front of it. He wrote a sentence, then deleted it with a deep exhale. Then he removed the rest of the paragraph while he was at it. It simply wasn't good enough. He couldn't really get into his work recently. Something was bothering him. An unease was stirred inside the pit of his stomach, but he didn't know why. Something just wasn't right. Was it some sort of sense of impending doom? It felt like it.

Dr. Milton shook the thought and returned to his article. This was all just nonsense. He only felt uneasy because this was the most important article of his entire career. If he did this one right, he would be remembered for many years after his death. It would become his legacy, one he could be very proud of.

It wasn't until he heard the creaking sound coming from behind him and turned to look that he realized it might be too late. As the knife penetrated his neck, his last thoughts were of regret that he had been too slow to write the darn thing.

Now, no one would ever get to read about his life's greatest work.

It had all been in vain.

Chapter 33

I LEANED back in my chair and tapped my stomach. "Wow, that was really good. I ate the entire thing."

Alex looked at my empty plate, then grinned. "You want some of my pasta too? I can't eat it all."

I sat up straight. "Are you implying I'm fat? I will have you know that I lost seven pounds recently. I've been dieting."

He shook his head. "No, I would never. I think you're perfect."

"Oh, really? Do say more things like that."

Alex laughed and emptied his glass of wine. The waiter came by and poured more into both of our glasses. This was a nice restaurant. The waiters were just as snooty as the detective at the police station, but maybe that was just the way they were up here. I wondered. Perhaps it was the French in them? They did try and speak a lot of French to me, but I quickly let them know I didn't understand a word of it.

On the other hand, Alex was—of course—fluent in French and just yapped away with them like there was no tomorrow. It made me feel inadequate and a little left out. But once the food arrived, it was so worth it. It was the best pasta dish I'd had in years. It was going to punish me on the scale later on, but hey—we got to live too, right? Can't stay off carbs forever. At least I know I can't.

Once the waiter had left, I sipped my wine and looked at Alex. I was probably getting slightly buzzed by this time because I suddenly found him even more attractive than before.

But I wasn't ready to go down that road. I hadn't decided if I wanted to be in a relationship or not yet. I was doing really well on my own, to be honest, and enjoying being alone with the kids. I used to think I could only be happy if I was in a relationship with a man, but lately, I realized I actually enjoyed my own company. It was freeing somehow not to have to worry about some guy's feeling all the time—to watch whatever I wanted on TV at night, and eat whatever food I liked. So, needless to say, I wasn't totally sold on the idea of dating Alex or anyone else for that matter. Yet he was very insistent, and I found that attractive. And yes, I also had needs that I sometimes succumbed to.

Could it be that maybe I just wanted to date and not necessarily be in a relationship? But was that even a possibility?

Alex looked into my eyes and leaned forward. He reached out his hand and put it on top of mine. It became awkward, even though I enjoyed it. I didn't say anything. He kept looking at me while sipping his wine with the other hand.

'This is nice," he said.

"Don't forget we're working," I said and pulled my hand out of his. "I have an important day tomorrow. Hopefully, this guy will talk to me."

"What if he is just some random dude and not the father?" Alex asked with a smirk.

"Then we go back," I said. "Emptyhanded."

"And what if he is? What do you expect to get out of him?"

"I want to know the story. What happened to the twins? When were they separated, and why? Where has the other girl been living all this time, and who is she? Does he know her name? My theory is that she grew up with him and came down to look for the rest of her family when she was brutally murdered."

Alex nodded and sipped more wine. "Sounds like a good story for my book."

I scoffed. "It's also peoples' lives we're talking about here. Don't be insensitive."

I waved at the waiter and signaled to get the check. As he nodded and left, Alex leaned forward on his elbows.

"I didn't mean to be."

I cleared my throat. I was too buzzed to think clearly, which wasn't good. I needed to get to bed before I did something I might regret later.

"Where is that waiter with the check?" I grumbled. "How can it take this long to print out a piece of paper?"

"You're cute when you're annoyed; has anyone ever told you that?" Alex said, finishing his glass.

I looked at him, then started to laugh.

"That's not a very good pick-up line," I said.

"Really?"

"Trust me."

The waiter brought the check, and I pulled my credit card out of my purse and handed it to him.

"No, this one is on me," Alex said and handed him his card instead.

"Alex, I can pay for my own food."

"Well, now, I am paying for it," he said, mocking me. "What are you going to do about that?"

The waiter left with the card, and I grumbled, annoyed again.

"I need to set something straight with you. This is not a romantic trip, Alex. We're not on vacation together. I brought you here because you wanted to follow my work so you can write about it."

"That doesn't mean we can't have a little fun while doing it," he said with a huge grin.

One part of me wanted to punch that grin off his face; the other wanted to kiss those soft lips.

"I'll just... I'll go to my room," I said and got up. The room was spinning slightly. I hadn't drunk wine for quite some time, so it really got to me.

"You don't want to grab a drink in the bar?"

I shook my head, even though I really wanted to go. I had to be careful. "It's an important day tomorrow, and I can't be tired."

"Okay," he said and threw out his arms. "I totally respect that. I will see you tomorrow for breakfast."

"Yes, see you tomorrow."

I turned around and rushed out of the restaurant, hoping he didn't notice that I was blushing.

Chapter 34

THEN:

"I thought someone had broken into our house!"

Tom lifted the baseball bat and approached his mom. Seeing the rage in his eyes, Raina became paralyzed with fear. What if his mom was right? What if she had told her the truth? Was he a murderer? Would he kill his own mother?

Would he kill Raina? The children?

"T-Tom, settle down," his mother pleaded. "It's just me."

He turned to look at Raina, eyes ablaze. "What were you two talking about? *Why* are you talking to her?"

"S-she was in here when I brought Noah back in. I swear; I didn't know she was your mom until she told me. I got scared and thought... I worried that she might hurt the children. But then she said who she was and I...."

"You shouldn't have talked to her," he said and pointed the bat at Raina.

Raina whimpered and took a step back.

"Tom, don't hurt her," his mom said.

He turned toward her, pointing the bat at her. "You get out of here. Now. I will literally count to three, and if you're not out by then, I will kill you. And I don't ever want to see you again. Do you hear me?"

"But, Tom... I...."

"ONE..."

The old woman whimpered and hid her face in her hands. "I'm sorry, Tom. I am just... please understand why I...."

Raina felt awful for the poor woman. She was completely devastated. This was her own son, threatening her. Was that really necessary?

"TWO..."

The woman turned to look at Raina. The look in her eyes made Raina almost begin to cry.

"Listen, my dear; I am telling the truth here. You must be careful. And with the children too. Please. Take care of yourself. Keep an eye on those kids. Keep a close eye on them."

"I will," Raina said, nodding.

"THREE..."

As he said the last number, the old woman slid out the door and was gone within seconds. Raina stood back in the nursery and stared at Tom and the baseball bat in his hands. His nostrils were flaring, and his eyes were on fire.

Then the bat came down.

"I'm sorry," he said. "But now you know why I didn't want you to meet her. The woman is crazy as a bat."

Raina forced a smile. She looked at her husband, but he seemed different to her now. She had never seen such anger in him before.

"She... is?"

He exhaled. "Did she give you that old crazy story about me murdering my sister and her going to jail for it?"

"Y-yes."

"Argh, I'm so sick of her. You can't believe her, Raina. She's not well. She's been in and out of mental hospitals all my life because she can't tell the difference between fantasy and reality. It happens when she stops taking her meds, which is quite often because she hates taking them."

"But the things she said...."

"Listen, Raina. She came here in the middle of the night and snuck into our kids' bedroom. If that isn't crazy, then I don't know what is. She scared the bejesus out of both of us. Why couldn't she just have come here during the day?"

Raina stared at her husband, and her shoulders came down. Both kids had woken up, and Tom grabbed Noah, then tickled him lovingly till he laughed instead. Raina felt overwhelmed with guilt for having believed the woman, even if it was just for a second. After all, his story did make more sense than hers.

"So... she's crazy, huh?"

"I told you. Mad as a bat."

"I sure hope it doesn't run in the family, heh," Raina said, then grabbed Charlotte and looked at her beautiful face.

Chapter 35

MONT TREMBLANT HAD my heart from the second we approached it. No cars were allowed downtown, so we had to park and walk the rest of the way. The town looked very European with its small businesses on small, quaint cobblestoned streets. There were lots of restaurants and bars for the many skiers once they were done for the day and came down the mountain—and also small clothing stores and ice cream shops.

"Who eats ice cream in thirty degrees?" Alex asked when we passed one. An elderly lady in an apron served a soft serve covered in thick chocolate to a young girl, handing it to her through a small window.

I shrugged. "I do. What's wrong with that?"

He shivered. "It's too cold. I want something warm, like burning hot chocolate or coffee."

I nodded. "Or maybe all of it. Ice cream and hot chocolate, but together."

He shook his head with a grin. "You're impossible. But it's cute. Where are we going again?"

The cobblestone streets were wet from the melted snow, and

my boots were slippery. I almost fell a few times before we reached the main square.

"It should be right over there," I said and pointed at a small red brick and stone building. "The address says he lives above that pub there."

"He lives up there? That must be awful with all the people coming and drinking after skiing."

I shrugged again. "Maybe he likes that."

"He has shown us he isn't a family man; that's for sure."

"Technically, we don't know that," I said. "She could have thrown him out, or maybe they took one child each. It's happened before. Maybe she just didn't want Meg to know she had a sister, and that's why she kept denying it."

"Do you think the mom might have killed her?" Alex asked as we approached the entrance to the building.

"I keep wondering about it," I said and looked briefly at my soaking wet boots. "But I also keep asking myself the question, why? Why would she do it?"

"To protect her secret."

I wrinkled my nose. "But is that enough of a motive?"

"Could be to some. People have killed for less."

"Good point."

I pressed the button on the intercom and held my breath. This was it. This guy could tell us he didn't want to see us, and then there wouldn't be much we could do about it. The Montreal Police Department hadn't been of much help, to be honest, and I had no real jurisdiction here.

No one answered.

"Do you think he might be at work?"

"Maybe," I said and pressed the button again.

Still, no answer. I sighed.

"What do we do?" Alex asked.

I looked at the pub. It seemed to have just opened.

"Let's go talk to them in here. If anyone knows the people living in this town, it'll be the people working here."

I walked in and sat down at the bar. A tall man approached me behind the counter. He asked me something in French, and I looked at Alex. Alex said something back, and the guy brought us two sodas.

"You're American?" he asked. "What brings you here if not for skiing?"

I showed him my badge. "Official business."

"Looking for someone around here?" he asked with a grin.

"Yes," I said. "The guy who lives upstairs in the apartment above this bar. What do you know about him?"

Chapter 36

THE TALL BARTENDER shook his head and put down the glass he was drying with a towel. He looked at his feet, then back up at us.

"I don't really know him, to be honest. I have seen him around, of course. You know, come and go, but he mostly keeps to himself."

"You don't happen to know where we can find him right now?"

He shrugged. "He could be on the slopes, like everyone else at this time of day. Or maybe he works somewhere in town? I don't really know. Why do you need him?"

"We just need to talk to him. Something happened to one of his children, back in Cocoa Beach, Florida, where we're from."

The bartender paused. "Children? What happened to his children?"

"His daughter was killed. We suspect foul play."

He put the glass down, and his eyes glared at me.

"Murdered? But... that's awful. H-how?"

I was observing him. Something was off. His movements had changed after I asked about the man living upstairs. They were slower now, like he was thinking about them and about seeming normal. His vocal tone had risen too—just slightly. It wasn't so much that it was obvious, and it could just be the nervousness about talking to the FBI, which usually threw people off a little.

But it could also be something else.

He could be lying to us.

"Tell me... what's your name again?" I asked. "I don't think you told us."

The bartender stared at me. "Maybe I can ask in the kitchen if anyone knows him. Let me just check."

He turned around so fast that I couldn't protest. He took off into the back of the bar.

"He was suddenly in a hurry, huh?" Alex said. "That's odd."

I bit the inside of my cheek. "I have a bad feeling about this. Something is off with this guy."

I glanced toward the door where he had disappeared while tapping my fingers on the bar counter.

"What are you saying?" Alex asked.

I took a deep breath, still looking at the door, waiting for it to open and his face to show. When it didn't happen, I felt myself get agitated. I looked at Alex, then got down from my barstool and approached the door.

"I'm saying I think he has run."

I pushed the door open, and as I did, I spotted the guy at the end of the kitchen just as he exited the back door.

"Hey!"

I ran through the kitchen, then reached the back door and pushed it open. I went outside in the snow, my eyes scanning the area, when I spotted him just as he disappeared around the corner of a building. Alex came up behind me.

"What do we do next?"

"What do you mean 'what do we do next?'" I asked. "Isn't it obvious? We go after him."

As I said the words, I started sprinting across the street toward where I had seen the bartender disappear. I reached it and spotted him as he ran across the road toward the ski lifts, pushing his way through the crowd of people waiting in line to get on the gondola.

I followed after him, thinking the people would slow him down. I was right, but soon I was going through the same crowd, and they weren't exactly being helpful. People yelled at Alex and me, even though I lifted my badge and yelled FBI. I had to use my elbows quite a bit to make it through, and just as I spotted him again, he jumped inside the gondola the second it took off.

Chapter 37

WE JUMPED inside the next gondola as it moved past us. I sat down while it started to move, anxiously watching the gondola above us with the bartender inside. I could see him looking nervously back at us from inside of it.

"This gondola goes to the top," Alex said, looking up at the mountain in front of us. "He can't escape us from up there. There's nowhere to go."

"I hope you're right," I said and looked down at the treetops below us. We were getting up high now, and I wasn't very fond of heights. I felt a tickling sensation in my stomach as we were lifted higher and higher, and the ground below became distant. "Oh, dear Lord," I said.

"What? You're afraid of heights?" he asked.

"No, just of falling from them."

He chuckled. "Who would have known? The famous bad-ass FBI agent can't take heights. Have you never skied?"

"Actually, I did when I was younger, but it's been like twenty years. And I don't mind the skiing part; it's the *dangling-in-the-air-to-get-there-part* that I am less fond of."

"So, how did you manage to be in the lifts back then?" he asked. "I take it you were afraid of heights back then as well?"

"Closing my eyes," I said and did just that.

The mountaintop approached us while my heart began to race in my chest. I accidentally looked down at one point, opening my eyes just a crack, and that set me off. My heart was racing rapidly in my chest, and my fingers started to tingle.

I hadn't always been like this—it was like it was getting worse with age. Maybe it was just because it was so long since I had been in one of these. I didn't like the feeling of getting more scared of things with age. It annoyed me and made me feel old.

You can do it, Eva Rae. You can. You're being ridiculous.

The gondola started shaking in the strong wind gusts, and I gasped lightly. I opened my eyes just in time to see it enter the end station. I looked out the window and saw the guy just as he jumped out of his gondola in front of us.

"There he is. Let's not lose track of him," I said.

Our gondola made it into the station, and we jumped out. It felt good to have solid ground beneath my feet again. I spotted the guy as he hurried toward the restaurant up there. I set after him. He ran toward a row of ski racks where people had parked their skis while they went to eat at the restaurant. He passed that, then hurried to a shed, where a snowmobile was parked outside of it. He jumped on top of it, started it up, then turned around fast, blowing cascades of snow toward us, then took off.

"Holy moly," Alex said, panting, as we dusted the snow off of us. "I did not see that coming."

I looked at him, then scanned the surroundings. I hurried toward the shed and pulled the sliding door open.

"Bingo!"

Another snowmobile was parked in there, probably belonging to the ski patrol. I jumped on it, then started it up. It roared to life. Alex stared at me.

"Are you sure you're allowed to do this?" he asked.

I revved the engine. "Who cares? Do first—ask later," I always say.

Alex kept staring at me without blinking. "Oh, that's good stuff. That's going to be in the book. That's excellent."

"Really?" I said. "That's what you're thinking about right now?"

"That's always what I'm thinking about," he said.

"Well, stop thinking so much and jump onto the back."

"Yes, ma'am," he said with a grin, then did as I told him. A second later, we roared out of the shed and onto the slope going downhill.

Chapter 38

MRS. MILTON WAS A REASONABLE WOMAN. At least she believed so herself. She didn't expect much from her husband, as he had been very direct with her from the beginning that she would be in charge of the children. And she had been. Yet, she still felt like she was getting really tired of his attitude toward them, and she had decided it was time to have a chat with him about it. It was okay that he didn't want to do all the work that came with them; that was the agreement. But the least he could do was accept the fact that they were there; they were a part of his life and living in his house. They should be allowed to make some noise, play, and even fight because that's what kids did.

"You need to create some space for them in your life."

That's what she had decided to say to him. She had spent the entire afternoon at the park with the kids, hoping they'd get tired from all that running around, so they might settle down a little and not make as much noise once they got back to the house. Louise Milton knew that her husband had a very important article that he was writing, something about it being his life's project. She didn't know any details, as he never wanted to share anything with her.

Probably because he thought she wouldn't understand. But in reality, Louise was a lot smarter than he gave her credit for. She understood a lot more than he thought. And she had taken a look at his research papers some weeks back and been quite astounded by what she had found out. She wasn't completely sure what he had discovered, but he seemed so excited about it that she concluded that it had to be significant.

Louise held her children's hands as they walked back toward the house, hoping that Dr. Milton would have finished his article by now, so they could all relax together. She didn't like it when he got all tense and yelled at the children because of it. It wasn't their fault that he wasn't done with it yet.

"Maybe Mommy and Daddy will share a bottle of champagne later on," she said, addressed to the kids, who didn't react. "Maybe he will take me celebrating. Someplace nice."

Louise smiled to herself at the very thought of her finally getting to put on one of her nice dresses again and seeing him in his suit—one of the black ones she would put out for him to wear. They'd call the babysitter who lived down the street. Maybe they'd stay out until midnight.

"Maybe we will even go dancing, huh? How about that?"

The kids still didn't seem to understand what she was talking about, and she didn't mind. She longed for adult companionship and conversation and hoped that she would get to do that soon. She hoped that her husband would receive awards for his work, and then they would go to some of those fancy parties that they used to before she had the kids—back when they just met.

She missed those days from time to time, and she could tell he did too.

But she was also so happy to have children. She really was.

"But Mommy's gotta have some adult stuff in her life as well," she said as they reached the driveway, and she let go of their small hands so they could race to the doorstep. She opened the door, and just as she did, she heard the back door slam shut.

Louise wrinkled her nose.

"What was that?"

She hurried to the kitchen window and looked out the back, just in time to see a shadowy figure run across the snow on their lawn.

"What was that, Mommy?" her daughter asked while tugging at her pants.

"I don't know, sweetie," she said and lifted the girl into her arms. "I don't know."

"Maybe it was a robber?" the girl said.

"Yeah, maybe he got disturbed when we came home," Louise said, feeling anxious. She hurried to the living room and opened the door to the study.

"Honey, did you see someone...?"

She stopped in her tracks. She just stood there while the kids tugged at her arms, yelling and screaming her name.

"Mommy, Mommy! What happened to Daddy?"

Louise wanted to scream too, but for some reason, she couldn't. Instead, she sunk to her knees, sobbing.

Chapter 39

HE WENT DOWN the black diamond. Of course, he did. And I had no other choice but to follow him. As I approached the crest of the hill, I realized I was in way over my head here. I knew how to ski down a mountainside but not ride a snowmobile. The thing sort of just took off downhill, and I completely lost control. Alex was screaming in the back while I went down so fast that my hands were shaking.

"Turn! Turn," he yelled behind me, clutching onto me from behind so hard it hurt my ribs.

Finally, I managed to turn the snowmobile sideways and got it stopped in some deep and heavy snow. I breathed heavily as it came to a full stop.

The guy was already halfway down the slope, and I studied him to see how he did it, then followed. I had to bring the snowmobile on edge and, while sticking my leg in the snow, tip it to the side, leaning into the hill like I would on skis. That worked like brakes just well enough for me to slow down and regain control. Then I could sort of carve it from side to side, getting us down the steep hill.

But the bartender was so much faster than us, and soon he was nothing but a small dot on the horizon.

"This is going too slow," I said.

"W-what do you mean?" Alex whimpered.

"Hold on tight," I said, then turned the nose downward and let it go straight downhill once again.

Alex screamed loudly behind me while I focused on steering this thing, my hands hurting from holding so tight and my butt throbbing from all the bumping. As we reached midway, I lost control again. The thing skidded sideways, and we ended up in the snow. I tried to rev the engine, but it wouldn't.

"What's wrong?" Alex asked.

"I… I think we're stuck."

"Try again."

I did, and it coughed a lot, then spurted snow everywhere before it got loose. We took off once again, full speed ahead going down. We soon made it to the bottom, but the bartender was nowhere to be seen. I couldn't even spot his snowmobile anywhere.

"That sucks," Alex said as I turned off the engine and got off. We left the snowmobile and started walking into town again, going past the bar to see if he might be there, knocking on the door to the apartment again, but with no luck.

"I'm afraid he got away," I said.

"Do you think he was the dad?"

I looked around me, scanning the town. People were in the streets now, filling them, wearing puffy ski clothes and heavy boots. They had been skiing all day, and now it was time to go shopping or drinking downtown.

"Eva Rae?"

I looked up at Alex. "I don't know. But I did get a photo of him when we met him in the bar. I took it with my phone without him seeing it. I say we hand it to the police in Montreal. Have them work a little and pay off their debt to the Chief."

Chapter 40

THEN:

For years, they did well. Raina was able to put the incident with Tom's mother behind her and move on. She didn't hear from her again, yet from time to time, she thought about her and whether or not she was okay. She wondered if they should have done more to help her instead of throwing her out the way they did. Where was she now? In a mental institution somewhere? Living in the streets?

Who took care of her?

She so wanted the twins to have a relationship with Tom's part of the family, and when the twins had their second birthday coming up, Raina had an idea. One she, of course, brought up with her husband first since she was the type who always considered his feelings above everything else.

When she entered, he was sitting in the living room, watching some house-flipping show on TV. The twins were down for their nap, and Raina felt exhausted because Noah kept pulling his sister's hair forcefully while they took their bath before naptime. It was like the toddler found great joy in hurting his little sister, and his eyes almost lit up when he made her cry. Raina had desperately tried to teach him that it wasn't appropriate behavior and to be good to his sister.

"Brothers always tease their little sisters," Tom would say when she brought it up on occasion. "They love torturing them. It's perfectly normal. I used to do it to my sister all the time."

It wasn't often that he mentioned his sister, and when he did, Raina so desperately wanted to ask him what happened to her. He had never told her, and she didn't know if she was alive or not. Was the story his mom had told her partly true? Had the sister been killed? Raina didn't dare to ask. She feared his reaction if she did. He hadn't exactly reacted calmly when she brought his family up earlier.

Yet now, she approached him and sat down, ready to face him.

"Honey, I've been thinking."

"Mm-hm?"

She placed a hand on his knee. "Honey, will you look at me?"

He did but was visibly annoyed. "What is it?"

"I've been thinking about something."

His eyes returned to the screen. "What about?"

"Well, the twins' birthday is coming up and…."

"Yes, I know that. You have that big party planned with all the balloons and flowers, and you even have a clown coming, even though everyone knows how terrified most children are of clowns. I'm not gonna forget that so easily."

"Yes, yes, that's right, but there is also something else. You know how my parents are both coming, and my uncle and his grandchildren and… well, several of my old friends who also have children about the same age and…."

"Yes, you told me all this already. Raina, what is this about?"

"Well… I was thinking that most of the guests… no, make that *all* of the guests are either family or friends of mine. Don't you want to invite someone?"

He stopped watching TV, then looked at her, mouth frozen. "What's that supposed to mean?"

"I was just thinking, why don't we invite someone from your family?"

"Like who?"

"Like your mom… or your… sister?"

Tom stared at her. He wasn't blinking.

"T-Tom?"

His nostrils were flaring, and the look in his eyes terrified her. Tom rose to his feet, and Raina pulled back. He stared at her, a vein popping out on his forehead.

Then he turned around on his heel and left the house, walking into the snow without even taking a coat or closing the front door behind him.

Part IV

TWO DAYS LATER

Chapter 41

SEAN ANDERSSON LOOKED at the gas meter in the car. It was blinking and had done so for quite a while. This wasn't good. He needed gas, and he needed it fast. This was the third car he had stolen since he left Mont Tremblant, and it had a full tank when he took it, but now it was already running low. Sean was terrified of stopping at a gas station, where they might have cameras. He didn't dare to use his credit card either, in case they were tracing them. He would rather change cars again. It was also safer if he didn't stay in the same car for too long. It made it too easy for them to trace him, which he assumed they had tried to ever since he left the bar in Mont Tremblant and lost the FBI on the slopes.

He knew they weren't going to let go of him that easily.

Sean took the nearest exit from the highway and found a small town. He drove down what he assumed had to be the town's main street, or maybe the town's only street, then parked next to a blue Toyota pick-up truck.

If this has a full tank, it should be able to take me the rest of the way.

He looked around, then got out of his car. It was getting

warmer now as he was moving further south. He had taken his time, staying off the bigger roads, but he was steadily making his way down there. He had stopped at an internet café on the way and read about the murder of the young girl in Cocoa Beach, Florida. He learned she was found at the bottom of a pool of her own mother's house, even though that wasn't where she lived, and the police still didn't know where she came from or where she had been beforehand. They asked the public for help to identify the girl and only knew that it was her mother's house due to a DNA profile.

The cause of death was stabbing, it said. They had found five stab wounds in her chest. As Sean used his wire to open the door of the pick-up truck, he wondered a lot about that very detail. It seemed quite interesting to him and slightly puzzling. In fact, there was a lot he didn't quite understand about this story, if he was being honest.

A lot.

He picked the lock, then entered the truck and crawled underneath to remove the plastic cover on the steering drum with the screwdriver he always carried with him for emergencies like these. He got the wires out, and seconds later, the display lit up, and the engine started.

Sean stared at the gas meter. He was in luck. It was almost full. He figured he had another six hours or so left to Cocoa Beach, so hopefully, this truck would be the last one he would have to steal.

Sean backed out of the parking lot, then swung the truck into the street just as a guy—who he believed could only be the truck's owner—came out from a restaurant nearby. He was waving his arms widely, then running toward him. Sean didn't stop or slow down. He roared the truck forward and ran it toward the man with no intention of stopping. The man waved eagerly and yelled something that Sean couldn't hear and didn't care what was either.

In the second he was going to hit him, the man threw himself to the side of the road and landed in the grass. Sean didn't even care enough to look in the rearview mirror to see if the man had gotten up.

Chapter 42

"HE GOT AWAY FROM US."

"He got away from you? How is that possible?"

Matt stared at me across the meeting room at the new police station. Alex and I had just returned from Canada the night before. Emptyhanded. And now we were explaining it all to the team that Chief Annie had appointed to work on the case.

This wasn't a good feeling at all.

I leaned back in my seat with an exhale. "He ran when we started to ask questions, and we set after him but lost him. I provided the local police with a picture of him I had taken at the bar where he worked, and all they could tell us was that his name was Sean Andersson and that he was known locally by most people because he worked at the bar and lived in the apartment above it.

"So, is he the twins' father or what?" Matt asked.

"We still don't know that," I said. "They had no records on him or any DNA we could use to try and do a match."

I paused and drank coffee before I continued. "I would have stayed and looked for him, but the border patrol had footage of him crossing into the United States about four hours after I lost him on the slopes. He must have gone directly there before I could get his picture out to the police and border patrol. The car he was driving was stolen and later found outside of Albany. That's where we lost track of his whereabouts. I came home instead."

"Wow, so nothing, huh?" Matt said.

"I'm sorry I wasted precious time on this," I said. "I had a hunch and followed it. But I didn't get anything out of it. I wasted everyone's time."

"You don't say," Matt said, throwing out his hands. "Well, at least you got to go on a trip with your boyfriend on this department's expenses. That must have been very nice."

I stared at my ex-boyfriend sitting across the table from me. What was his problem? Was it just jealousy?

"Wow," I said. "Bitter much, Matt? I will have you know that Alex paid for his own ticket and food while there. It didn't cost your department anything. And he's not my boyfriend. He's writing a book about me."

Matt rolled his eyes with a scoff.

"Yeah, right."

I slammed my hand on the table. "Why are you being like this, Matt? Why can't you just...?"

Chief Annie cut through. "Now, let's not fight here. Eva Rae's hunches are usually very good. We can't win them all. We need to focus on what we're doing next. I, for one, would love to talk to the mom again. She needs to explain some things. Where are we on her?"

I nodded. "I know where she is hiding. I can go talk to her."

Chief Annie smiled. 'Take Matt with you."

I paused. "What? Why?"

She lifted both her eyebrows. "Because I say so."

"I am perfectly capable of...."

"I don't want you going there alone, and Matt has nothing else to do today, so there you have it. It's not up for discussion."

Chapter 43

THEY WERE MAKING out on Meg's couch. Trevor moaned in her ear, then kissed her again. His hand crawled down her neck toward her breasts. He tried to reach inside her shirt when she stopped him.

"Not now, Trev."

He looked disappointed. "Why not?"

"I just don't really want to." She pushed him away, and they both sat up. She corrected her shirt and her hair. Trevor groaned.

"You never want to be with me anymore."

She gave him a strange look. "Is that really so weird? I'm kind of going through a lot of stuff here."

"I know; I know. A sister you didn't know, dead in the pool, and a dad you haven't spoken to in forever."

"Wow, you make it sound like I'm overreacting," she said.

"Well, maybe you are a little bit," he said. "You take things so seriously. You didn't use to. We used to have fun, remember?"

"My world has kind of crashed, and you think I'm taking it too seriously?" Meg said. "Who says something like that?"

Trevor grinned. "I'm sorry. I didn't mean anything by it. I just miss being with you; that's all."

"Shouldn't you be in class, by the way?" she asked. "At community college?"

"Shouldn't you?"

She made a face. "You know they gave me time off, so I can grieve the loss of my sister."

"A sister you didn't even know you had," he said.

"It's still a sister."

"Barely."

"What?"

He shrugged. "It's just... how can you grieve the loss of someone you have never spoken to?"

She sighed. "Okay, that's it. I'm gonna need you to leave. I can't deal with you right now."

"But... babe?"

She pointed her finger at him as he tried to grab her around the waist. "Don't! Don't touch me, Trevor."

He gave her a surprised look. "Okay, wow."

"Just... just leave, will you?"

"What's wrong with you?" he asked. "It's me... Trevor?"

She turned away from him, then sighed. He placed his hands on her shoulders. "Babe? What's the matter?"

She turned to face him. Their eyes locked. "It's just...."

"What? Babe?"

"The other day... you had a knife in your truck? Why did you have a knife in your truck?"

He shrugged. "For fishing. You know me and Bobby like to go fishing."

"Ah... okay... well, of course."

He shook his head with a deep exhale. "I don't believe you. Why would you ask me that? Do you suspect me or something?"

"Well... no, I just...."

"I can't believe you," Trevor said, walking away from her. "You think I killed your sister? Because of a knife in my car? Every kid around here has a hunting knife to gut the fish we catch. If you suspect me, you might as well suspect Bobby or any of the other boys at the party that night. I can't believe you."

He was in her face now, yelling at her, and Meg took a step back. His eyes were angry, and his gestures aggressive.

"Besides, do you really think I would be stupid enough to leave a murder weapon out in the open for everyone to see if I was trying to get away with murdering someone?"

"I... I don't... know...."

He lifted his arm, and Meg bent down, afraid he might hit her. He paused when seeing her wince and cover her head.

"You're unbelievable; do you know that? How do we know that you didn't kill her, huh? You're so busy pointing fingers at everyone else. Maybe you killed her, huh?"

Meg closed her eyes in fear but heard footsteps and opened them again just in time to see him walk away. He grabbed the handle to the front door, opened it, and slammed it shut behind him.

Meg then hurried to her room, found the card that the FBI woman had given her, and called the number on it.

Chapter 44

"I JUST CAN'T–FOR the life of me—understand what you see in this guy. He is not your type at all."

I put the car in park outside the beach house on Sixth Street. I wanted to scream. Matt had been going on all the way there about how he had to take care of our child Angel while I was on a trip with my boyfriend, how it wasn't fair to him that he had to constantly throw everything he had in his hands whenever I needed it and take care of her. It was just one thing after another. And now he felt like that was all he was to me after all these years.

A babysitter.

I turned to look at him, exhausted from all his ranting. "Well, it's a good thing you don't have to understand. See, you're not the one going out with him. I am."

He paused. "So you *are* going out with him? I thought you said he was just writing a book about you?"

I rolled my eyes. "He is."

Matt shook his head, and we both exited the car and then began to walk toward the yellow house.

"I don't understand. Are you or aren't you dating this guy?"

I stopped in my tracks, then turned to look at him. "Matt, you and I are history, remember? I don't think I owe you any explanation."

"Oh, really? But this guy might be around my daughter, and I can't have a say in that?"

"How many women have you dated since we broke up?" I asked. "Let's see, there was Tabitha, Maureen, and Laura, and then there was Sandra, and... Giselle, right? Am I forgetting anyone?"

"That's beside the point," Matt said but lowered his voice to almost a mumble. He knew I was right but refused to admit it.

"I really struggle to see how," I said.

"That guy... Alex... he's... he's...."

"Go on. Say it."

"He bugs me, okay? I don't like him, and I don't want him near my daughter. There. I said it."

Matt walked past me up to the front door on the side of the house. It was a two-story beach house big enough to house several families.

I rang the doorbell, then knocked.

Nothing happened.

I tried again—still nothing.

"She's not here."

"Or maybe she just doesn't want to talk to us," I said, then walked around the house to the back. The ocean was rough, and it was windy on the beachside. I stepped onto the back porch, then stopped.

"The sliding doors are open," I said.

I peeked inside, then called her name. "Susan? Susan Kellam? This is Agent Eva Rae Thomas and Matt Miller with Cocoa Beach Police Department. Can we come in? We just want to talk to you."

The curtain was swaying, and I realized there was a draft. Somewhere, another place in the house, a window or another door had been left open. It could be to cool the house down, but not in this Florida heat?

I put a hand on my gun, feeling anxious. It wasn't just the draft that had me worried. It was also the blood I spotted on the white tiles inside.

Chapter 45

THEN:

Tom was gone for three days before he finally returned. Raina had almost given up hope of ever seeing him again. She was feeding the little ones when he suddenly walked through the front door. She almost dropped the bowl of grits she had made for the twins when he suddenly walked in. He was wearing different clothes and had a plastic bag in his hand.

"T-Tom?"

Raina stood to her feet. She had been sick with worry and had wondered if he might never come back.

Tom stared at her, then smiled. "How about I make us some pancakes? Are you hungry?"

Her eyes grew wider, and her heart hammered in her chest. Should she ask him where he had been? Why he left? Did she dare to?

You might scare him away again.

Raina cleared her throat. "Y-yes, that would be great. I'm starving, actually."

"Pancakes it is for my love, then."

Tom smiled, then rushed to the kitchen, where he started on his endeavor. Raina couldn't remember if she had ever seen him cook before and worried he had gone mad.

What if he burns down the house?

But all her worries were soon put to shame. Tom served her the pancakes, then sat down and ate with her, acting as if nothing had ever happened—like she had never asked him about his sister and he had never left.

"You like them?" he asked when they had both taken a couple of bites.

Raina cut a pancake for the twins to eat using their hands, sitting in their high chairs. Noah gulped down his, then reached over, stole his sister's, and ate that. Charlotte started to cry, and Raina moved her chair so Noah couldn't reach, then cut up another pancake for her.

"They're delicious," she said, trying to put a smile in her voice. "I didn't know you knew how to make pancakes."

He stopped chewing, and Raina felt a chill run down her spine. Had she said something wrong?

"I... I mean I...."

Tom reached over and grabbed her hand in his. He squeezed it, and it felt like it was a little too hard. Then, he smiled again.

"It's about time, then, huh? From now on, I will make pancakes every Sunday morning for my lovely wife and kids. How does that sound?"

Raina breathed calmer when realizing that he wasn't angry. She was terrified of him leaving again. Three days alone with those two kids had been exhausting. Especially since she hadn't slept much at night, worrying about Tom and where he was and being mad at herself for asking him that silly question when she knew he had a hard time talking about his family.

"That sounds amazing," she said.

He got up, put his arm around her shoulder, and then pulled her close to his chest. "There's nothing like family, huh?"

"You're so right, Tom," she said, relieved. She realized then that she didn't need to know where he had been or why he got so upset. He was here now, and they were all together.

That was all that mattered.

Chapter 46

"THIS DOESN'T LOOK GOOD."

I glanced up at Matt while kneeling next to the trail of blood on the tiles.

"It's not fresh," I said, touching it lightly with the tip of my finger. It didn't stick to it. "Whatever happened here happened days ago, if not more."

"I'm calling it in." Matt grabbed his phone and walked outside while I studied the living room and open kitchen. I walked to the counter. A bloody hand had left a print on the edge.

"Like someone was grabbing it and holding on to it, trying to get up," I mumbled to myself. A splatter of blood on the wall behind caught my attention. "And then another stab fell, perhaps the second one, and the person stabbed tried to drag herself...." I followed the bloody trail that could only have been made by someone dragging their bloody body across the floors, trying to get away from someone.

A lamp had fallen from an end table onto the floor. There were bloody fingerprints on its sides. I looked at them, then at the lampshade that was pushed flat on one side. The bulb inside was shattered. There was blood on it too.

Hopefully, it belonged to the perpetrator.

"I think whoever was harmed in here, and my guess is that it was Susan, managed to fight off her attacker over here, using this lamp," I said when Matt came back inside still with the phone in his hand.

"And then the trail of blood continues this way, toward the sliding doors," I continued. "And there was a bloody handprint on the curtain too."

"You think she grabbed it to try and get up?" Matt asked.

"Probably, but that's when the third stab fell. Look at the amount of blood on the floor over there, and there are more bloody fingerprints on the glass door."

"This is nasty," he said.

"The trail of blood ends by the doors but doesn't continue on the other side."

"And what do you make of that?"

"My fear is that she died by the door and that the perpetrator put her over his shoulder and carried her outside, and maybe into a car in the driveway. We need to ask neighbors for surveillance cameras. Houses like these on the beach almost always have them."

"We're on that for sure."

He paused and looked out at the ocean. "Do you think Susan Kellam is dead?"

I swallowed hard, not quite knowing how to answer that. "After three stabs with a knife? It's very likely."

He looked at me.

"But *you* don't think she died?"

I bit the inside of my cheek. "I have this weird tendency to think people are alive until I have seen their dead bodies. Call me crazy, but that's just me."

My phone was vibrating in my pocket, and I took it out. The number calling was unknown. I picked it up.

"Hello?"

"H-hello?"

The voice was young and seemed fragile. I recognized it immediately. "Meg?"

She cleared her throat. "Yes. It's me. I… need to talk to you. It's about Trevor; you know my boyfriend?"

"What about him?"

"I… I don't know. I just… what if he killed my sister?"

"And why would you think that he did that?"

"I don't… I don't think it… it's just…."

"Meg, have you found something?"

"A knife. He has a knife in his car, a big one. And he… I don't know… it's just the way he is so fascinated with my sister's death, almost like he enjoys it. I don't know. I might be wrong."

I stared at the blood in the room around me, then felt my heart break for the young girl. "Meg, I need to talk to you too. It's about your mom. I'm afraid I have some bad news."

Chapter 47

"EXACTLY HOW LONG DOES SHE have to stay here with us?"

"I don't know, okay? She's in pretty bad shape still."

"Honey, we don't know where she came from or what happened to her. She could be in some sort of trouble. We should call the police or take her to the hospital at least. Then they can take care of her."

Susan could hear their voices as they cut through the fogginess that had been her mind lately. It was hard for her to distinguish if this was really happening or if it was all just a part of her dream.

"I told you she came here asking for my help," the male voice continued. "The last thing she said before she passed out was not to tell anyone where she was and not to take her to the hospital or call the police. I have to honor that wish."

The female voice groaned. "What if she is involved in something bad? Who doesn't want to go to the hospital or the police when they've been stabbed? I'll tell you who. Criminals. And you let that inside of our house, where our children live, into our family. We might get in trouble, Brad. Don't you see that?"

"I do, but... I couldn't just leave her out there. She was bleeding. I was afraid she might die."

"Oh, so I guess it had nothing to do with the fact that she's your old girlfriend, huh?"

"We went out for a few months some years ago before I met you, Lisa. I think she came here because she knew I was a nurse and because no one would look for her here. She's in trouble somehow, and I can't turn a blind eye to that. It doesn't matter who she is."

"Gosh, you are impossible," Lisa growled.

"I'm sure she'll wake up soon," he said sternly. "Then we can ask her what is going on. I refuse to bail on her now."

Susan tried to open her eyes, but the lids wouldn't move. It was like being in one of those dreams where you realize you're asleep and you want to wake up, but no matter how much you will it, it just doesn't happen.

Where am I? Who are these people that are talking?

Susan tried to remember what had happened, and slowly images came back to her. The beach house, the fresh ocean breeze on her face, and then something else. A shadow. A face. Someone was there.

Holding a knife.

Susan felt herself get agitated and started tossing in the bed she was in while images of the knife coming toward her rushed through her head. It was like waking up from being drunk the night before and remembering all the stuff you had done but had no control over. Only this was worse.

This was someone trying to murder her!

Susan remembered the lamp hitting the person's face and the person being pushed back. She remembered making it to the sliding doors and grabbing the curtain when this person, this man, grabbed her legs and pulled her forcefully. Then another painful stab in her back, and screams. Her own screams. And then what?

Susan opened her eyes and stared into the ceiling of the guest bedroom where she was staying.

I escaped. Then I escaped. But how?

The anchor!

There had been an old anchor by the door as part of the beachy decorations. She had swung it at the person trying to kill her. It had worked. The anchor had hit their shoulder, and the person had been pushed off of her. That's when she was able to run.

Oh, boy, how she ran.

"You're awake?"

Susan didn't recognize the man peeking inside the door to the room at first. He belonged to another time in her life, but as she stared at him, it slowly came to her.

"B-Brad?"

He smiled and came inside. A woman stayed in the doorway, arms crossed.

"Yes, that's me," he said. "How are you feeling? You lost a lot of blood. I took some from the hospital and gave it to you. I'm sure I will be in trouble for that, but let's cross that bridge when we get to it, huh? The most important part is that you're better."

"You didn't tell anyone I was here, did you?" she asked, her terrified eyes pleading with him.

He shook his head. "No. Not a single soul. You told me not to, remember? Right before you passed out. We almost thought we lost you."

Chapter 48

"I NEED a missing person's alert to go out, and I need it yesterday."

I stared at Matt, who was sitting by his desk at the Cocoa Beach Police Station. I was standing in front of him, worried out of my mind for Susan's safety.

"I'm working on it," he said. "But I need the chief's approval, and I can't get ahold of her. She's speaking at this fundraiser at the country club, but I've sent a patrol to get her."

"I don't like this," I said and bit my nails. "The blood on the floor in the beach house. There was a lot of it. I need to know if anyone has seen her these past few days. I want the media to post her picture everywhere, so anyone who might have seen her can come forward, even if it is her dead body being dumped somewhere. I need to know. She could also be bleeding out in a ditch somewhere."

Matt's phone rang, and he picked it up, then chatted with someone for a few seconds before hanging up again. He looked up at me. "They got ahold of one of the neighbors to the beach house. They live in Idaho, so this is their second home."

"I don't need their life story," I said. "Just tell me if they have cameras."

Matt smiled. "They do. It's on the side of the house that over-looks the neighbor's side. They're sending footage over for the past week; then, we just need to go through it all. I'll get one of my men to do that."

"Have him look for any movement at all, anyone walking or running past; even if it's a freaking raccoon, I want to know."

Matt nodded. "Yes, ma'am."

"What I just don't understand," I said. "Is why hasn't she tried to contact her daughter, Meg? I spoke to her earlier, and she hasn't heard from her. That's what worries me more than anything."

"Maybe she's scared?" Matt said.

"It tells me that she might be on the run from someone, maybe the same person who killed her other daughter and that she knows who the killer is."

"But you're thinking she doesn't want to lead the killer to Meg? She wants to keep her out of it?"

"Wouldn't you?" I asked. "Wouldn't you do everything to protect your other daughter in a situation like this?"

"Sure."

"It's either that or she is in such bad shape that she isn't able to contact her. That's also a possibility."

Matt nodded, then clicked with his mouse while staring at the screen in front of him.

"Or there is also the chance that she is dead."

I looked down at him, then shook my head. "I choose to believe people are alive until I see a body. That's just how I'm wired."

"I have always admired that about you," Matt said. "How you remain positive until the end even with all the scary stuff you have witnessed."

I paused and wrinkled my forehead. "Did you just give me a compliment?"

He shrugged. "I guess so."

That made me smile.

Matt's phone vibrated, and he looked at it.

"Finally."

"Chief Annie?" I asked.

He nodded and took it. "Chief. Glad you could get back to me. We need to move on this ASAP. We need the media involved."

Chapter 49

THEN:

"There's someone on the phone asking for you."

Raina held the landline out toward Tom just as he walked down the stairs. He looked at it, then up at her, eyes questioning.

"It sounds important," she added. "You better take it."

When he still didn't move, she tilted her head and gave him a stern look.

"It's the police, honey."

She handed him the phone, and he put it up against his ear.

"Yes? This is he."

A silence followed, and he nodded. "Mmhm.... mmhmm.... yes, well, okay...no, no, it's fine, yes. Well, thank you. Thank you so much for calling. Bye now."

He hung up; then, without looking at Raina, he walked past her and into the kitchen. She followed him in there and watched as he grabbed a cup and started to pour himself some coffee while humming to himself. He sipped the cup while Raina stared at him. The twins were napping upstairs, and she was really worried that they would wake up, so she spoke with as low a voice as possible.

"Who was that?"

He looked at her, wrinkling his nose. A frown grew between his eyes. "What do you mean? You know who it was."

"Yes, it was the police. But why were they calling you?"

He sipped his coffee and stared out the window while humming that same song again.

She shook her head and took a step closer.

"Tom?"

He turned his head to face her, then smiled. "Yes?"

She threw out her arms. She couldn't believe this. What was going on here? Why was he pretending like it was no big deal?

"Sweetie. The police just called our house. Are you not going to tell me why they called? What they wanted?"

"Oh, that? No, it was nothing important, really."

He leaned over and kissed her forehead. "Don't you worry yourself about anything. You have enough on your plate."

"Are you for real?" she asked. "You don't think that you not telling me why they called will make me worry even more?"

He put the cup down, then chuckled. "You're being silly, honey. Listen, it was nothing important. I mean it."

She put her hands on her hips.

"Then why don't you want to tell me what it was about? If it wasn't anything important?"

"Because it really was very uninteresting; that's all."

He walked past her, emptied his cup, then put it into the sink. She stared at his back, feeling a great unease spread inside her body.

"Tom, just tell me why they called, please."

He turned to face her again, then shrugged with a smile. "It was just to tell me that my mother had died. That's all."

He gave her a peck on the cheek, then walked past her with a shrug, humming that same song again.

Raina thought she had heard him wrong. She had to have, right?

"Excuse me?"

"What?"

"Did you just say that your mother died?"

He smiled and nodded. "Yes. Someone found her in her house, dead."

Raina's eyes grew wide, and she wasn't blinking. "You're telling me that your mother is dead, and you're not even sad about it?"

He nodded again. Yeah."

He was about to leave the kitchen when she put a hand on his shoulder to stop him. He turned to face her again.

"Wait," she said. "I need to straighten this out. You're telling me your mother, the woman who birthed you and raised you. You're telling me she is dead, and you're... happy?"

He shook his head, and, for a second, she thought that maybe he was just still in shock and that she had misunderstood him. He placed his hands on her shoulders, then said:

"Sweetie. It's not like I liked her very much."

Then he let go of her shoulders, turned on his heel, and left the kitchen, humming loudly.

Chapter 50

I HAD TURNED on the TV in the police station's break room and was zapping through the news channels.

"Still nothing," I grumbled. "I can't believe it. Why is it taking them so long?"

Alex had come in to follow my work for a few hours and was sitting with his coffee at the table, scribbling in his notebook. He was annoyed with me for not telling him about going to the beach house earlier. He wanted to have the scene in his book. But I told him we just went there to pick up a person of interest. I had no idea we'd run into a crime scene. I had promised I'd take him down there later, so he could at least get some of it in his book or maybe recreate the event. I wasn't sure I had the time for it, though. I was very set on finding Susan Kellam. I believed she was alive somewhere, and I was so worried about her.

"You need to be patient," Matt said, coming into the kitchen to grab an apple from the fruit basket that a local produce store had sent over for us as a generosity. "Things don't move as fast down here. Not like you're used to up in D.C. We did our part. We sent it all out; there's nothing more we can do."

Seeing Alexander sitting there, Matt paused in his tracks, and his lips went tight. Alex nodded in a greeting.

"Hey, man."

Matt barely looked at him. "Hey."

"Wait a minute," I said as they returned to the anchor after some silly report about the prices for tickets at Disney being raised once again. "It might come on now."

I turned up the volume, and the anchor introduced a new story.

"Nope," Matt said and took a bite of his apple. "More on the gas prices that were raised again."

"Argh," I groaned. "How can that be more important than a missing woman who might be hurt?"

I stared down at Alex, who was scribbling in his notebook.

"Don't put that in your book," I said.

He looked up. "Why not?"

"Because... well... I want to come off as nice and not some impatient crazy woman who yells at the TV."

He shrugged. "It shows your passion for your work."

Matt scoffed loudly. "Ha."

"What's that supposed to mean?" I asked.

He bit the apple again and shook his head. "Nothing. Nothing. Say, the guy has sent over some clips that he wants us to look at from the neighbor's surveillance cameras. Do you want to go through it?"

I stared at him. "And now you're telling me? Yes, I want to see it. Why are we wasting our time yapping here?"

Alex grabbed his stuff and followed us just as I could hear the missing person's report start in the break room.

"The Cocoa Beach Police is asking the public for help in the case of a missing woman...."

I didn't hear the rest but rushed to Matt's computer. He sat down, clicked with his mouse, and opened a couple of files.

"This one is from the day she came to the beach house," he said. "Late in the evening."

"You already watched it?" I asked.

"Well, yeah. I wanted to make sure there was actually something we could use."

"You could have said something," I said.

"Geez, thanks, Matt, for doing the hard work, so I don't have to," Matt said mockingly.

He clicked on the file, and it opened.

"See, it shows someone walking past the camera at eleven fifteen p.m., and then fast forward to eleven thirty-two; here we see the same person again, rushing past the cameras. Now it's nothing but a dark figure who looks like they're wearing a hoodie, so we can't see a face, unfortunately. I don't know how much we can use this for."

I nodded. "That's not much, but there is one thing we can get from this. Look, this person isn't carrying anything or anyone as they leave the house, which means that Susan left the house on her own somehow."

"You're saying that Susan actually might be alive?" Matt said.

"Like I have said all along."

"Unless her dead body was buried in the backyard," Alex added. "Before this person left."

We both turned to look at him. "You can't kill someone and bury their body in twenty minutes. Besides, we had the dogs out on the property, and they would have smelled it, and the techs would have seen it if there had been any recent digging in the yard."

Alex lifted his hands. "Just mentioning it as a possibility."

"Yeah, well, don't," Matt said.

"Okay, so, just tell me how it is that we don't see Susan Kellam on any of these surveillance cameras, huh?"

"There could be a ton of reasons for that," Matt said. "That doesn't mean anything."

"But it could."

"Okay, you two," I said. "Matt is right, Alex. Susan might have gone around the other side of the house or ran directly onto the beach. The latter is the most likely as this was late at night, so she could easily hide in the beach's darkness—more so than if she ran into the street where all the lamps might reveal her whereabouts. If she was trying to get away from a possible killer, the beach was her best opportunity, and the cameras wouldn't see her there."

"Amateur," Matt said and played the video again. "Coming here telling us how to do our work. Stick to your little writings, buddy, and let us do the police work, okay?"

I ignored the two roosters and stared at the video on his screen. This person moved differently on the way back than on the way in.

"Go back," I said. "Go back again and play both clips."

Matt did, and I stared at it. "Look, there."

"What?"

"Look, this person is holding their arm as if it hurts. They're hurt."

Chapter 51

"HONEY? Brad? You have to come and see this."

Susan heard the wife yell while sitting up in the bed in the guestroom. She was eating soup. Brad was feeding her with a spoon, as she couldn't really lift her arm properly. Every sip she took hurt to swallow. It was like her entire body was broken, cut up, and nothing was working anymore.

Will I ever feel like myself again?

Brad smiled as she took another spoonful, wincing in pain. Even little movements hurt like crazy.

"There you go," he said and wiped her chin where a drop of the chicken noodle soup had run down. "This will make you feel better in no time."

"Brad?" Lisa called from the living room. "You need to come in here. I mean it. Come here now."

"I'm in the middle of something," he yelled back.

"No, you need to come now."

Brad exhaled and shook his head, annoyed. His focus returned to Susan. "Do you think you can get another one down?"

She nodded even though it hurt to do so.

"All right," he said excitedly. "That's what I like to hear. We're making great progress today. Here comes another one. Open wide."

Susan opened her mouth when Lisa called again.

"BRAD!"

He almost dropped the spoon on Susan when he jumped. Some of the soup was spilled onto the white covers. He wiped it off frantically.

"Oh, no, look at that mess."

"BRAD!"

"Maybe you should go see what is going on," Susan said, feeling tired. "I need to rest anyway."

He sighed, put down the bowl, and then wiped his hands on the dishtowel. "All right. I'll go see what she wants now. You rest, then you can have more of the soup later."

Susan forced a painful smile, then closed her eyes and put her head back on the pillow.

"Thank you," she mumbled while dozing off.

"BRAD!" Lisa yelled again, and Susan woke up. She saw Brad disappear out the door, leaving it open so she could hear the TV in the living room.

"I told you so," she could hear Lisa say. "I told you she was trouble. This woman is wanted by the police. Person of interest, they say—in a murder case. We can't have her staying here. We have children, Brad."

"But… Lisa, honey… she's in need of care…."

"I don't care if she needs a new kidney. Get her out of here, please. I can't stand the thought of harboring a fugitive."

"I hardly think she's a fugi…."

"Just get rid of her, Brad. Will you? Or I swear I will take the kids to my mom's and call the cops on you both from there."

"I was hoping we could wait until she feels a little better," Brad said, but Susan could hear in his voice that he knew the battle was lost. She tried to move in the bed and managed to swing her legs over the edge, even though it was very painful. Brad came in and saw her, then ran to her side.

"Oh, no. You're not ready to get out of bed just yet."

"I heard you and your... wife," Susan said while panting in agitation. "I know when I have overstayed my welcome. I will get out of your hair now. The last thing I want is to cause you trouble. You've been so good to me."

"But... but where will you go?"

She bit her lip and looked up at him. "That's what I need to find out. Now that there's a county-wide search out for me, there really aren't many places to hide anymore."

Chapter 52

TREVOR MCCOY LIVED in a beautiful two-story Mediterranean-style house by the golf course. I drove up into the driveway, parked in front of the garage, and then walked to the front door. The bell rang loudly inside, and I felt like I was about to visit royalty.

His mom opened the door, and I showed her my badge. She got a terrified look on her face.

"The FBI? What's going on?"

"I'm just here to talk to Trevor, please."

"My son? Why? What did he do?"

"Your son is in no kind of trouble, ma'am. I just need to have a word with him," I said.

"Oh, okay," she said.

"Can I come in?"

"Yes, yes, of course. Excuse the mess, but we're reconstructing the pool area in the back."

I shook my head and followed her inside, closing the door behind me. "I don't mind at all. I'm not the cleaning police."

She laughed, but it was so nervously that I knew it was just because of who I was and the circumstances. It wasn't because she liked my joke.

"Trevor? Son?" I heard her say as she went into the kitchen. She had pointed at the dining room table and told me to sit down before she went to look for him. I looked out the arched windows overlooking the pool and, behind it, the golf course. The workers were setting up a new screen on the porch in the back, surrounding the pool area, keeping out the mosquitoes.

"Here he is," she said and pulled Trevor out of the kitchen by his arm.

He winced.

"Trevor," I said. "Sit down for a second. I just need to have a chat with you."

"Do you want me there?" his mother asked.

He shook his head.

"He's nineteen, right?" I said. "He's an adult."

"O-okay," she said. "I'll be right in here if you need me, okay?"

"Okay, Mom," he said, annoyed. He sat down at the table across from me. "So, what's up?"

"Thank you for taking the time to talk to me. Now, you're not in any trouble, okay? I just have to ask you a few questions. Is that okay? I will record everything; I hope that's okay with you."

"S-sure," he said.

I placed the recorder in front of us and said my name and who was present. I told him to state his name for the record, and he did.

"All right, Trevor," I said. "Now, you previously gave the statement about your whereabouts on the night of the party on the eighteenth of March. Could you please repeat it for me?"

"Do I have to?"

"Please, it would be of great help to us."

He exhaled. "All right. I came to Meg's house around nine

o'clock along with my friend Bobby. There were a bunch of people already there, hanging out by the pool."

"Was there alcohol involved?"

He paused. "Yes, I have already said that before. We were drinking beers, and someone had brought vodka, so we took some shots. I got drunk and passed out on the floor in the living room around three a.m. Later on, when I was helping clean up, I heard Meg scream for help and ran to see what was going on. I jumped in the water and pulled out the body with Bobby's help. Then, someone called the cops; I believe it was Abbi, but I'm not sure."

I nodded. That was all consistent with his earlier statements. He wasn't giving me any signs that he was lying.

At least not so far.

"Okay. Now, it has come to my attention that you are in possession of a knife in your truck; is that true?"

Trevor paused. "Excuse me? Is that what this is about... did... did Meg... oh, my God, I'm gonna kill her." He paused, then looked at me, terrified. "I don't mean that literally, of course."

I cleared my throat. "I'm gonna need to take that knife with me to get examined. Can you get it for me?"

His eyes grew wide. "But... I don't have it anymore."

"And why don't you have it anymore?"

"After Meg said those things, I thought... I worried that I might get in trouble, so I dumped it at the inlet. I threw it in the river."

I stared at him, scrutinizing him. "Now, why would you do that if you have nothing to hide?"

"I... I don't know, I just... I didn't want to get in trouble. You hear all these stories of people going to jail for something they didn't do, and then...."

"But if the knife was no match and didn't contain any evidence, it would serve to clear you instead," I said. "Can you see what I am saying?"

He stopped talking and was staring at me, eyes wide. "I... I don't know what to say now."

Silence broke out between us, and I noticed he was rubbing his arm. "Is something wrong with your arm? Or your shoulder?"

He moved it. "It's just a little sore; that's all."

"From what if I might ask?"

He hesitated, which made me listen extra carefully for what he said next. And how he said it.

"Just... from the gym. I went this morning and lifted weights; I guess I did too much."

"The gym, huh?"

He nodded, but his eyes were wandering, and the tone of his voice was raised as he said the next words.

"Am I in trouble?"

I smiled and closed my notebook. "Not yet. But I wouldn't leave town if I were you."

Part V

ONE DAY LATER

Chapter 53

NOT KNOWING where else to go, Susan spent the night on the beach and slept in the dunes. She had no money, so she couldn't leave town, and she didn't dare to go back to her friend Tina since she knew she was wanted all over, and she feared getting her in trouble.

Also, she was pretty sure that the killer would only find her there. If he knew to find her at the beach house, he would have no problem finding her at Tina's house. In fact, both the killer and the police would probably expect her to go there and were most likely watching the house.

Susan sat on the soft sand and watched the sun rise above the Atlantic Ocean, its rays glistening in the crashing waves. It was gorgeous but already getting hot out. A guy had set up three fishing poles by the shore and sat in a chair, watching the sunrise while smoking a cigarette. Susan felt how she began to sweat and could smell herself. She desperately needed a shower and looked down at the clothes that the man-nurse had given her; they probably belonged to his wife. Susan had bled through the shirt, and the pants had dirt and stains on them. If it was mud or blood, she couldn't tell, but they really needed to be washed. She realized she had to look just like those homeless people that usually hung out on the beach in front of the Beach Shack, getting drunk with whatever was in those brown bags they always carried. She used to shake her head at those people and pull her daughter away from them when they passed them.

Now, she was one of them.

"Guess it's true what they say," she mumbled to herself while digging her fingers into the sand next to her and letting it slide out between her fingers. "Karma really is a...."

She stopped herself when she spotted a woman she knew, Allison. She worked as a personal trainer at the local fitness center and always went running on the beach at the crack of dawn. Susan never liked her much, but their kids had been friends for a little while, and the two of them had hung out. But then the kids had grown apart, and Susan hadn't seen this woman in a long time.

Allison wasn't alone this morning. She had a group of women with her, all running. As they came closer, Susan realized they were all moms from the high school where Meg had gone.

Susan's heart stopped.

I can't let them see me like this!

She could hear their voices as they came closer and rose to her feet. But it was too late. Allison had spotted her and called her name.

"Susan? Is that you?"

Susan started to walk faster through the dunes. Allison ran up close.

"It *is* you. Susan, where have you be...?"

Susan paused. She didn't want to turn around and face this woman while looking like this.

"Susan, they're looking for you... the police...."

"Just leave me alone, will you?" Susan said, then continued to walk away.

She began to run, even though it was so painful with the wounds that were still healing. She reached the overpass, then slowed down when she realized Allison wasn't following her. She had gone back to her flock, and they continued their run, probably all chatting about Susan and how deep she had sunk.

Susan tried not to care.

She walked up to A1A, then continued down toward the small shops. She stopped in front of the Italian pizza place and stared in the window, feeling so hungry she could cry.

The owner stepped outside and sent her a look that made her lower her head and rush away.

A crowd of beachgoers that wanted to get a good spot on the beach in the early morning approached her, and she bowed her head even further, then walked through them, sensing how they pulled away and made space for her, probably because she scared them. They almost recoiled in disgust—just like she used to do.

So, that's what it's like being on the other side.

She accidentally stepped on a woman's sandal, and the woman shrieked in pain.

"I'm sorry. I'm so sorry," she said and rushed away.

Susan tried to run, but it was painful, and she turned the corner to the square in front of Coconuts. It was already swarming with people going to the beach, and she saw faces everywhere; then, she rushed down a small alley behind Hunkerdown Bar, where she paused and caught her breath.

She would bet that Allison had already posted in *Let's Go Cocoa Beach*, the local Facebook group, that she had seen her, and soon the police would come looking for her.

The thought made Susan want to cry and just surrender herself. But she couldn't. The police would have to know the truth, and she couldn't have that. She couldn't face that right now.

In fact, she probably never would be able to. It was simply too unbearable—too darn hard.

"I gotta find somewhere to hide," she mumbled to herself, then turned around the corner and went into the parking lot and crossed it. She came back onto A1A and crossed the street when someone came toward her. She didn't see his face as he was wearing a jacket with the hoodie pulled up over his head. He bumped right into her, almost knocking her over. As he did, he stuck his hand inside her pocket.

Susan fell back and yelled out for help, but the guy was fast and ran away. People walked around her in the street, not even caring that she was hurt.

They probably think I'm just another drunk. Heck, I would have felt the same just a week ago.

Susan got back up and realized she was bleeding from one of her wounds in the abdomen, soaking her shirt. She leaned up against the wall to Woofgang Bakery, the local dog bakery, and closed her eyes when her hand felt the thing in the pocket that the man had put there. She pulled it out and realized it was a small note. She unfolded it and read the words:

YOU BETTER RUN

Gasping for air, she stared at the note and read the words over and over again. Then, she crumpled it up, tears springing to her eyes, and threw it on the pavement. She looked around her to see if she could spot the person who had given it to her, but he was long gone. She took a few deep breaths, then turned on her heel and started to run, pressing through the pain shooting through her body.

Chapter 54

WE ALL OVERSLEPT. I woke up with a gasp, then realized it was almost ten o'clock, and the kids weren't awake yet. I ran from room to room, waking up first Ollie, then Christine, and Alex, and rushed into the nursery, where I found Angel sitting in her bed, babbling along while playing with her Minnie Mouse stuffed animal that Matt had given to her when he took her to Disney. I smiled, relieved, then grabbed her in my arms and took her down to the kitchen, where I fed her, then whipped up some quick breakfast for the bigger kids, who soon came storming down the stairs one after another, backpacks in their hands. I threw them all in the minivan, then rushed them to the schools. Luckily, Roosevelt Elementary School, where Alex went, was right next to the high school and middle school where the two big kids went, so it only took like seven minutes to get them all dropped off. There was a lot of yelling and arms gesticulating, but finally, I got them all shipped off, and I could breathe again.

I hated these types of mornings. I just couldn't believe how we could all miss our alarm clocks. I always told Ollie and Christine to make sure they set one, too, just in case. But for some reason, we all slept right through them. Or maybe we all forgot to set them. I know that's what happened to me. Usually, I didn't need one because Angel would wake me up, but apparently, this morning, she just decided she wanted to play on her own and not demand my attention.

That was a first.

I drove her to preschool and dropped her off in the arms of one of the teachers, then rushed to the police station, grateful to live in such a small town that all this could be done in just a few minutes.

Except when I drove into the parking lot, I realized I was still in my PJs. I had just stopped the engine when seeing this, and it made me laugh out loud almost manically inside the car. Then I started it back up, drove home, and got changed before going back there again.

Matt was waiting for me as I entered the building.

"Where have you been?"

I realized I hadn't turned my phone on at all yet since I had been so busy getting the kids out of the house. I hadn't even thought about it.

"I've called you an insane number of times."

"I'm sorry," I said and rushed past him toward my desk. "It's been a morning; I can tell y'all that much."

"Your boyfriend Alex is here," he said, walking after me. "You left me alone with that guy all morning. He kept asking me all these questions. I don't want to be in that stupid book. Can you tell him that?"

I nodded. "Okay. You're not interesting enough anyway."

I winked at him, and he made a face.

"Very funny. Now, get your things together; we need to go."

"Where are we going?" It was Alex who asked the question coming toward us with his messenger bag slung over his shoulder.

I smiled when seeing him. He was so handsome. He always

made me happy, even when he was being annoying. I don't know why.

Matt rolled his eyes. "We received a call on Susan Kellam's whereabouts," he said and showed me a post-it note with an address on it and a name. "We need to go talk to them."

Chapter 55

THEN:

She couldn't get the thought out of her mind. Raina stared at her husband while eating breakfast and winced as he slurped his coffee.

Why wasn't he sad that his mother had died?

Raina mulled it over and over again and couldn't—for the life of her—understand him. She knew he didn't like her. Yes, that became very obvious when he threw her out of their house that night she came to visit Raina.

And told you that your husband killed his own sister!

But not to be the least bit sad that she was gone? That wasn't something Raina could wrap her brain around. You heard about people who had even suffered abuse as children, and still, they were sad the day their parent died, even if it was the abuser. It was still his mother, for crying out loud—no matter what. And yes, Raina did understand that his mother was a little—let's put it nicely—mentally challenged, but was that her fault? She was sick; she needed help.

Raina shook her head and tried to get rid of the thought. It had been two days since the call came, and it was all she had been able to think about. She didn't even know if they were going to the funeral or when it would be. She didn't dare to ask any of those questions, and sort of hoped Tom would answer them without her having to ask.

He will tell me when the funeral is, right? Or is he just planning on ignoring it?

Raina bit into her buttered toast, her eyes still lingering on Tom. She felt so oddly nervous around him lately and was always careful what she said and cautious about how she acted when he was there.

Raina chewed her food, then washed it down with coffee before grabbing the cup and plate and taking it to the sink.

"I'm gonna go do some laundry," she said. "Could you look after the twins?"

Noah and Charlotte were both sitting at the table, drawing. Tom didn't even look up from his phone but just nodded with an *mm-hmm.*

She stood there and looked at the kids anxiously for a second. She didn't like leaving him alone with them much, but she was just going to be doing laundry in the garage. It should be fine.

As she was about to leave the kitchen, she glanced out the window, and her eyes fell on a cop car as it drove into their driveway.

She wrinkled her forehead and watched while two men in civilian clothes approached. She could see their badges attached to their belts as they moved toward the door.

"T-Tom?"

He got up and looked out. The two men knocked. She went to open the door, but Tom stopped her. "I got this. Don't worry."

"B-but... why are they here?"

"I said I will take care of it," he said, then pecked her on the cheek before walking to the front door.

She stood for a few seconds listening in and heard them present themselves as detectives. Her heart knocked against her ribcage as she saw him close the door behind him and walk outside to talk to them alone, ensuring she couldn't hear any part of the conversation. She tried to look at their faces and read their lips or gestures to figure out how serious this was. But she couldn't really see anything, and Tom stood with his back turned to her.

Maybe he just doesn't want you to worry?

Maybe it's nothing?

She decided it was probably okay, then looked at the twins, still peacefully drawing as if nothing had happened.

A few minutes later, Tom returned, a smile on his face. "I gotta get ready for work."

She got up. "Excuse me? You're not going to say anything?"

"About what?"

Is this guy for real? Is he kidding me?

"The police were just here, Tom. Detectives. Do you mind telling me what this was about?"

"Oh, don't get yourself all twisted again," he said dismissively. "You always do this. You worry too much."

"Well, maybe I would worry less if you told me more."

She glared at him, not standing down this time. He kept dismissing her, telling her not to worry, but how could she not?

"Oh, you silly woman," he said. "It was just some formality concerning my mother's death—some paperwork needed to be signed. That's all. It was nothing. Don't worry about it. Say, have you seen my blue shirt? I really want to wear it to today's meeting. I looked but couldn't find it anywhere. Do you know where it is?"

She stared at him with a deep exhale. He really wasn't going to get into details, was he?

It's probably nothing to worry about. His mother died; of course, there's a lot of stuff that needs to be taken care of.

But why by detectives?

Stop it, Raina.

"Raina? My blue shirt, the one with the black buttons?" he repeated.

"Give me a second and keep an eye on the twins while I look," she said and rushed upstairs to the bedroom while repeating to herself that, of course, it was nothing to worry about.

She went through his shirts on the hangers, found the blue one in the back, and pulled it out. As she did, she accidentally pulled out something else from the bottom of his closet. It was a plastic bag. She looked inside it, then froze to ice. Inside it was a shirt, a white shirt.

All covered in blood.

Raina stared at the shirt between her hands, unable to fathom what she was looking at when she heard footsteps behind her.

"Did you find it?"

She turned to look at Tom in the doorway, still clutching the bloody shirt between her hands.

Seeing what she was holding, Tom's lips became tight, and he slammed the door to the bedroom shut behind him.

Chapter 56

"THIS IS WHERE SHE SLEPT."

The tall skinny blonde woman named Lisa Marlon showed us into a guest bedroom. The sheets still had blood on them.

"My husband, Brad, is a nurse. He's been deployed to war zones three times and knows how to deal with wounds."

I walked inside and looked around. "You're telling me she came here, and you treated her?"

Brad Marlon nodded. "I knew her... a little."

Lisa growled and hid her face between her hands. "I told you we shouldn't have kept her here. We kept a murderer in our house, Brad. You brought her in here where we live with our children."

Brad looked at his wife. "I don't think...."

Lisa didn't listen; she turned to face me. "She's wanted for murder, right? That's what they said on TV."

"We're looking for her as a person of interest," I said. "That's all."

She put her hands at her sides. "For now. That just means you don't have enough evidence. But I tell you, she killed that girl in the pool, the one down in Snug Harbor. I know she did. I could see it in her eyes. She had those murdering eyes, like a mad man. And that's what you brought into our house, Brad. Into our home."

"She was hurt?" I asked Brad. "Was it severe?"

He nodded. "She had been stabbed at least three times. I treated the wounds and nursed her back to consciousness, but she is still in a bad state. She needs to go to the hospital. I just couldn't get her to do it. I couldn't turn her away either. I have vowed to care for people, and that's what I intend to do."

"Even if they are murderers?" Lisa shrieked.

He nodded. "Even so."

"Again," I interrupted. "She is not a suspect in the murder case. Just a person of interest. That means we are looking for her because we want to talk to her, not arrest her."

"Well, you should arrest her—fooling us the way she did. She probably stabbed herself for all I know," Lisa said. "To trick us into helping her, to gain my stupid husband's sympathy enough to hide her here."

I smiled at Brad, suddenly feeling all kinds of sympathy for him. Then I closed my notebook.

"All right. And you say you have no idea where she might have gone? Did she mention any names of people that she might go to?"

He shook his head. "No, to be honest, I got the feeling she had nowhere to go after this. I fear she might be out in the streets, bleeding to death. She was in really bad shape. I'm rather worried about her, to be honest."

"We'll do our best to find her," Matt said and shook Brad's hand. "Thank you for letting us know."

We left the house and walked back to the car. Alex was following closely on our trail, and I could tell it annoyed Matt.

"So, do you think the mother killed her own daughter?" Alex asked as we reached the car.

I exhaled and opened the door, then said:

"She does like to hide from us, and she really doesn't want us to find her; that is very suspicious. I'll give you that. But people have their reasons for doing what they do. Often, they have to do with the secrets they carry and try to keep buried. I have a feeling she is keeping one so big and terrifying that she might be willing to take it to the grave."

Chapter 57

HER FEET FELT SO HEAVY, and the stabbing pain in her abdomen was unbearable. Yet Susan continued to run down A1A, following the sidewalk, trying to get as far away from the man with the note as possible. She was gasping for air and holding her side while focusing on going forward and not stopping. Fueled by fear, she overheard all of her body's signals telling her she was in pain and in need of medical attention. One of the wounds had sprung open when she fell, and blood was soaking her clothes. It felt clammy on her fingers that were pressing on it.

You gotta keep going. He might be right behind you.

The heat was burning her throat, and it felt like her lungs were going to explode. Sweat dripped from her forehead onto her nose and upper lip. She felt so incredibly thirsty; it seemed impossible to continue.

I'm so... tired.

Finally, she had to stop as she reached the Chevron gas station in south Cocoa Beach. She simply couldn't run anymore, and she tumbled onto the grass on the side of the road while cars rushed past her. She saw stars dance in front of her eyes as she gasped for air, unable to breathe properly. She was certain she could literally feel the blood leaving her body and soaking the grass, creating a small pool. She felt so dizzy and tired, and it was hard to keep her eyes open, so she closed them, only meaning to do so quite briefly.

She didn't know if she had dozed off or been unconscious, but when she opened her eyes, someone was bent over her.

"W-wh...?"

The sun was behind him so that she couldn't see his face, but the hoodie pulled over his head told her everything she needed to know.

It was him.

Susan barely had any strength, but in this second, adrenaline kicked in, and she regained some, at least enough to kick him in the crotch. Her foot landed right in the good spot, and he flew back, cursing loudly. Somehow, Susan managed to get to her feet while he reached for her and grabbed her ankle, causing her to slam her face into the sidewalk. She kicked and screamed, then placed her hands on his face, pushing him away. Then, she kicked him again, got to her feet, and tried to run, limping forward.

"You won't make it far this time," he yelled behind her, getting to his feet. "You're hurt. You lost a lot of blood."

Panting, she looked down at her bleeding wound, then pushed forward as he came up closer behind her. She pushed herself as far as possible when he reached out his hand to grab her. Just as he did, she spotted a car coming toward her, then looked at his face.

"You will never get me," she said with a mocking grin.

"Oh, no, you don't," he said when he realized what she was about to do. He tried to reach for her, stretching out his arms, but it was too late.

Just as the car drove up next to them and was about to pass them, she jumped into the street.

Chapter 58

"SO, you're saying that we're nowhere, is that it?"

Chief Annie looked at me, arms crossed in front of her chest. She had summoned Matt and me into her office, and I knew she wasn't satisfied with our results. I couldn't blame her.

"That's not what I was...."

She leaned forward on her desk. "Come on, Eva Rae. You're better than this. Why do you think we call on you for help?"

I felt embarrassed.

Chief Annie sighed. "I'm sorry. It's been a tough few days. I'm being pressured from all sides—especially the media. They keep asking me who the girl is, and we still don't know. Where are we on that? A name? Anything?"

"We've heard nothing from the search for the father," Matt said. "We were really hoping he could help explain what happened to his children, if this girl grew up with him, or if they split them at birth and they grew up separately. It's been known to happen."

Chief Annie leaned back. "Yes, on that note. That's actually why I called you both in here. I just got off the phone with Montreal PD."

I stared at her. "They found him? They found Sean Andersson?"

She had a discontented look on her face, and I realized it wasn't good news. She folded her hands on her desk.

"Yes. They found him."

"They did?" I said, baffled because Annie didn't seem very happy about this news. What was going on here? What wasn't she telling us?

"That's great news. Where is he?" Matt asked. He looked briefly at me, then back at her. "Has anyone talked to him?"

Now, it was my turn to sigh. Reading Chief Annie's facial expression, I knew something was off.

"What?" Matt asked. "What's going on?"

"He's dead, isn't he?" I asked.

"What?" Matt asked.

Chief Annie nodded heavily.

"Sean Andersson," I continued. "They found him dead."

"Buried in the backyard of his townhome in Montreal," she said. "They tracked him to this place because he owned it, then went there, but found no one home. But then they brought in a K-9 unit that started digging where he was buried. He's been dead for at least ten years. Apparently, he was a loner, so no one missed him. He had no family, and he was retired. Neighbors thought he had moved and abandoned the house. It was a poor neighborhood, where not many paid attention. That type of thing."

Matt looked confused. "Wait a minute, how...?"

"Our man killed him and stole his identity," I said. "The bartender did; the guy we suspect is the father of the twins, the one that Meg called to warn. He then moved to the mountains with his new identity where no one would look for him and tried to stay hidden by keeping a low-key job."

"But why?"

"Usually, people do that kind of thing because they're hiding from the law," I said. "But the real question is, who is this guy really, and where is he now?"

Chapter 59

"IS this your first time in Cocoa Beach, Mr. Andersson?"

The tiny Asian woman behind the front desk at the Motel 6 stared up at him, eyes smiling.

"It's not, no," Sean answered.

"It is so nice here, isn't it?" she asked, eyes still smiling. "Sometimes, we almost don't want the tourists to know about it and come spoil it all, huh? We want to keep this place a secret."

She laughed at her own joke. Sean didn't. He just smiled politely while signing the paper she handed to him.

"Thank you," she said and took it when he was done. "So, what brings you here? You know someone here, maybe? You have family?"

He looked into her eyes, then nodded, hoping she would just stop all the silly questions and finish her job.

"Yes, I have family living here."

"Oh, I bet they're happy that you come visit, huh?" she said with an even bigger smile. "Lucky them."

She pointed her small finger at him, and he nodded while smiling through gritted teeth. If only she would hurry up and stop that incessant talking. Why were her lips still moving? Why was she snooping in his affairs? It was none of her business why he was here. Hadn't she heard of privacy? All she had to do was to renew the card to his room so that he could stay longer. Was that really so hard? Why did that require her to ask all these questions?

"I'm the one who is lucky," he said, then paused. When she looked confused, he added. "To be able to visit them in this beautiful warm place, with all the sunshine and the beautiful beaches."

She smiled again. "Oooh, yes, sunshine, lots of sunshine in Cocoa Beach. We're lucky to be here. So lucky."

"And I guess I am so happy to be here that I decided to stay another week," he said with a grin.

"You're more than welcome, Mr. Andersson," she said and handed him back his key card after running it through the slider.

He looked at it.

"Room 217 for another week," she added.

"That should do it. Thank you."

He walked out the door and spotted the stolen truck that had brought him there, then passed it and walked to the rooms. He found his, then placed the card on the reader, and it clicked open. Sean entered, then slammed the door shut behind him, breathing heavily.

You made it.

He was worried that they would realize that the credit card he was using to pay for this room was stolen by now, but apparently, the cards hadn't been blocked just yet. He still had time. And he didn't need much. He was almost done with what he came here for. There had been a few minor setbacks, but he would get there.

He was ready to finish what he had started.

Chapter 60

I GOT HOME to a house that looked like a bomb had gone off. I noticed that Alex's toys were spread out all over the living room while I picked up Christine's backpack and lunch box from the hallway and Ollie's oversized jacket from the floor in the living room. There were empty plates and bowls on the counters with half-eaten cereal, cups and half-filled glasses of sodas, and empty Gatorade bottles on the couch. Along with a pile of laundry that hadn't been folded.

Oh, dear Lord.

I had picked up Angel on my way home from the preschool, and she was crying—no, make that wailing—from my arm because I refused to buy her a toy that she wanted at Seven-Eleven on our way home. I put her down, and she crawled off while sobbing into the living room. I realized I was about to have a major drama queen on my hands.

I picked up a pair of pants from the floor, then folded them, but as I looked at the pile on the couch, I realized it was a little much. I found Ollie and Christine on the couches, feet up in the middle of the mess, watching one of the old *Scream* movies on TV.

They didn't even look up or say hello.

"Hey, guys? How about you clean up after yourselves at least?" I asked. "And put the laundry away?"

"In a sec, Mom," Christine said. "We just got to the good part. By the way, can we get a cat?"

"Yes! We want a cat," Alex said as he came running down the stairs. I kissed his forehead, then handed him a napkin so he could wipe the chocolate off his mouth that his siblings no doubt had given him so he would leave them alone to watch their scary movie.

"Can we, Mom, please?" Christine said, finally taking her eyes off the screen and looking at me. "We promise to take care of it."

"I'll feed it," Alex said, putting his hand up. "Then you guys can do the poop and pee."

He grinned at his siblings. Christine stuck her tongue out and yelled at him, "No way, Jose."

"Guys, will you look at this house?" I said, feeling exhausted. "We're not getting a cat. Remember what happened with the bunnies?"

They didn't answer. "Well, I do," I said. "I ended up taking care of them because you were all too busy when you lost interest. Then we gave them to that nice family with the two children, remember? I don't want that to happen again. You hear me?"

"But, Mo-o-om, a cat would be different," Christine said while someone got brutally stabbed on the TV in front of her.

"Guys, could you please not watch scary movies while the littles are in here?" I asked.

"Who are you calling little?" Alex said, placing his hands at his sides. He hated when I put him in the same category as his baby sister.

"You," Christine said. "Because you are so little."

"Am not," he argued.

"Are too," she said.

I rolled my eyes. It was like this *All. The. Time.* Constant bickering and arguing. It was making me tired. Mostly because I also had to deal with that kind of quarreling at work between Alex and Matt. They were just as childish. It was ridiculous and tiresome.

"Please, turn that off, or I will do it for you," I said, my voice getting stern. These kids were alone way too much lately, and it showed in their attitude.

Ollie picked up the remote and turned it off. I exhaled. "Finally. Okay, let's clean this place up, shall we?"

All groaned in unison. Now *that* they could agree on.

Chapter 61

THEN:

"W-what is this, Tom?"

Raina held up the bloody shirt. Tom walked closer slowly. Raina's breath turned ragged; her heart beat hard in her chest. She felt the panic as it rushed through her veins.

"Why do you have a bloody shirt in your closet?"

He stared at her, then took a few steps closer, reaching out his hands. "I cut myself doing yardwork."

"Yardwork? You never do yardwork, Tom, and why were you wearing your nice white shirt while working in the yard? I don't understand...."

Raina looked down at the shirt in her hands, then back up at him as he came closer. The way he looked at her made her feel uncomfortable.

"This is the shirt you were wearing when you left the house and didn't return for three days. Why is it suddenly covered with blood?"

"I told you," he said, sounding almost annoyed. "I hurt myself while working in the yard."

"But you don't do yardwork, Tom; why are you lying to me?" Her voice turned high-pitched and desperate. She could barely breathe properly. All she could think about was his mother. His poor little mother, who had been standing there in her nursery, trying to warn Raina.

"Tom? What is going on with you?"

He scoffed. "Nothing is going on with me. I might as well ask what's going on with you?"

He pointed his finger at her, placing it very close to her face, and she recoiled with a slight gasp.

"You're scaring me, Tom."

Raina took a step back, then one to the side, still clutching the shirt between her hands.

"Give me the shirt," he said. "Hand it to me."

She took another step sideways, moving away from him, trying to get closer to the door. She wasn't going to hand him the shirt, not in a million years. It could be evidence.

"I think I'm gonna keep it," she said. "And give it to the police."

He paused when she said it. His smile froze, and he stood still, clenching his hands into fists so hard his knuckles turned white. A fear-inducing look of furor in his eyes made her shiver and take another step toward the door. She was almost there. She could hear Charlotte crying downstairs.

"I need to... I need to get to the kids...."

"No, you don't," he said and reached for her, but she moved fast to the side so he couldn't grab her arm. He got the shirt instead and pulled at it hard. He held onto it until it ripped. She kept the bloody part and held it close to her body.

"Did you kill your mother, Tom?"

The question seemed to hit him like a smack in the face. His mouth turned downward, and his eyes grew mad.

"Give me that shirt!"

He yelled, then lunged at her with his fist first. Raina ducked just in time, and his hand went through the door, punching a hole in it. Raina shrieked when he tried to come after her once again. She grabbed the door handle and pulled the door open, slamming it into his face. He was pushed back, holding a hand to his bleeding nose, then he looked at it.

"You little...."

That's when she took off running. She almost slid on the small carpet at the top of the stairs as she jumped down, taking three steps at a time. Tom was quickly right behind her, grabbing her by the collar and pulling her back forcefully. Raina hit her back on the stairs and screamed. Tom came down on her, lifting his fist to punch again, but she pushed him, so he flew down the stairs, bumping his head the rest of the way, then sliding into the wall at the bottom. Raina rose to her feet and stared at him.

He didn't move.

"Tom?"

Still, no movement.

Raina didn't waste a second. She ran to the children, grabbed both of them in her arms, then stormed out the front door.

Chapter 62

I KNOCKED on Ollie's bedroom door and peeked inside.

"Can we talk?"

"I guess."

Ollie shrugged. They were sitting on their bed, a laptop on their knees, watching something on YouTube. I sat on the edge of the bed.

"What's up?" Ollie asked.

"Ollie, I expect more from you when I ask you to look after your little brother and younger sister after school. I need you to help out more. Step up your game. You're alone for a few hours after school every day, and you are the oldest. I can't come home to a house that looks like this."

Ollie scoffed. They looked up at me.

"I'm not a girl."

I wrinkled my forehead. "I know that. What does that have to do with anything?"

"See, that's the entire point. You don't know. You don't take this seriously at all. You keep treating me like one."

"What on earth do you mean?"

"Would you expect a boy to do all this? Keep the kitchen clean? Take care of younger siblings? Feed them?"

I stared at my child. They had a point. I probably would. But I didn't say that.

"This has nothing to do with gender; don't make everything about that," I said instead.

Ollie groaned. "But it is all about that, isn't it? My entire life."

"Why do you say that?" I asked, puzzled.

They paused. "Because I hate myself. I hate... this...." Ollie sat up straight and pointed at their chest. "These."

"Your... breasts?"

They were crying now. It broke my heart. "I hate them; I hate them; I hate them so much. I want to cut them off."

I really had to try hard not to get upset. This was rough, and I didn't understand anything anymore.

"But... these are yours; you were born with them... what if you want to have children one day?"

"I hate them so much, Mom. I want them gone. I should have been on puberty hormone blockers long ago. Then I never would have developed breasts or gotten my period. I should be getting testosterone, so my voice will grow deeper. I'm sixteen; I should have started the transition long ago."

"But why is it so awful to be a woman? I love being a woman," I said.

"Well, I don't. I just hate it, ugh; I hate it so much."

"Do you want to be a man?"

"Argh, haven't you been listening to anything I've said? I don't have a gender," Ollie growled.

"But then... what are you?"

"I don't want to be a man or a woman. I don't fit into any of those categories; I refuse to be put in those boxes. I want to be me. Just me. Not male nor female. Just me."

I took in a deep breath, trying to calm myself. I was getting very worried about the development of this conversation. I didn't like that they hated their body so much and wanted to make changes for life. I could deal with the name change, same with the loose and baggy clothes and the short haircut. But surgery? Hormones? It was all a little much.

"Okay, sweetie," I said. "I'm trying hard to understand it. You have to cut me a little slack here. I'm new to this."

"All adults say that. It's no excuse to be ignorant. Google it."

With that, they put their headphones back on and turned on the video, shutting me completely out. Saddened by all this, I got up and left the room. I went to my own bedroom and sat there for the rest of the evening, Googling and learning about Gender Dysphoria.

Chapter 63

SUSAN BLINKED. She felt groggy, and it was hard to focus. Someone was standing next to her, looking down at her.

"There you are," the woman said. She was wearing scrubs. "We almost thought we lost you."

"Where am I? What happened?"

"You're in the hospital," the woman said. "No, don't try to move. You've fractured bones in both legs and suffered lacerations to your left hip. Luckily, you had no bleeding to the brain, even though you hit the asphalt pretty hard."

"H-how?"

"It was a car accident," she said. "You were hit by a car. That's what they told me. You don't remember?"

"C-car accident? W...wha...?"

Susan paused as it came back to her slowly. The running, the hooded man, and then the... car.

"I'm not dead?"

The nurse shook her head with a smile. "No, silly. You survived. But it was pretty bad there for a while. Luckily, the driver wasn't going very fast when they hit you."

"But I was supposed to be dead," Susan said. "Do you hear me? I was supposed to die."

The nurse stopped smiling. She shook her head. "You need to rest now. Your body has been through a...."

"But I was supposed to die!" Susan almost yelled it, but the pain from the effort was too much. "I wanted to die."

The nurse looked concerned. "You wanted to die?"

"Yes. I wanted to leave this place for good."

"Are you saying you jumped in front of the car on purpose? That it wasn't an accident?"

Susan closed her eyes and tried to shake her head but couldn't. "Just leave me alone. Just forget what I said."

"I'm afraid I can't do that," the nurse said. "I need to talk to my superior about this."

The nurse left, but it was only a few seconds before she returned with a doctor. He looked at Susan, very concerned.

"What is this I hear?" he asked. "Did you tell Nurse Brown here that you jumped in front of a car on purpose?"

Susan stared at him. Were they going to make this into some big deal?

"It wasn't like a depressed sort of thing," she said. "I just didn't want to live anymore." She wondered if she should tell them she did it because she was running from someone who wanted to hurt her, but she kept that part to herself. She didn't want to make a big deal out of it all.

"That's it," she said. "It's nothing to worry about."

"Suicidal thoughts are very worrisome," the doctor said. "Nurse, alert the psych ward for an evaluation, and make sure she is kept under observation for the next seventy-two hours."

"It's not like I can go anywhere anyway," Susan yelled after the doctor as he left. "I have two broken legs, remember?"

The nurse looked at Susan, then tilted her head. "I'll stay with you until they get here from psych. We'll take good care of you. You're not alone in all this."

Susan groaned and closed her eyes, wondering how long it would take the killer to find her there. And this time, there was no way she could escape. With two broken legs, she couldn't run anywhere anytime soon.

All she could do was wait.

Chapter 64

"You need to be careful with that old dried-up well in the back-yard—so the kids don't fall into it."

Raina nodded. She was drinking coffee with one of the neighbors who had stopped by to welcome her to the neighborhood. She knew her townhome wasn't much, but it was the best she could get on such short notice and for as little money as she was able to get from her mother. It wasn't much, but it was a start—a fresh new beginning.

"To tell you the truth, it is actually the landlord's responsibility to have a thing like that covered up before you move in," the neighbor continued. Her name was Susan. "You should tell him to do that. I worry about those little ones there falling in. It's really deep."

"I will," Raina said, sipping her coffee. The twins were playing in the living room, and she was keeping a close eye on them from the dining table where they sat. They had been fighting non-stop since they left Tom and the house. Raina had stayed for a few weeks at a local shelter with them until they were able to move into the house. It had been the worst. Noah kept stealing Charlotte's toys and pushing her down until she started to cry. Raina couldn't stand it.

Maybe it was just the whole situation. Kids fought. It was normal. She was just so exhausted; it was becoming unbearable.

"I'm just so happy that we found something so quickly," she added. "I didn't even think about it, to be honest."

"Oh, I get it, girl," Susan said. "You don't need to tell me how it is. I ran from my husband fifteen years ago in the middle of the night too. Just let me know if there is anything I can do to help you get back on your feet. We women in this neighborhood, we stick together. We look out for one another. Someone messes with you; he messes with us."

Raina exhaled. "I'm really glad to hear that."

"So, has he been coming after you?"

Raina looked at Susan, then shook her head. "He doesn't know where I am."

"But he might find out," Susan said, then sipped her coffee and ate one of the cookies she had brought to welcome Raina. "Husbands tend to do just that if you run from them."

Raina nodded nervously. She felt a light shiver run down her spine at the thought of Tom finding her and the twins. She knew he would try. It worried her deeply. The look in his eyes when he tried to catch her in the bedroom had told her everything she needed to know about her husband.

He was a dangerous man.

The last time she had seen him, he was on the ground, unconscious but alive. She was certain he was back to his usual vicious self by now, but she didn't know how badly he had been hurt.

"So, have you thought about how to protect yourself?" Susan asked. "For when he does come looking for you?"

She hadn't. If Raina was honest, she had only thought about getting away and finding somewhere to live with her children. And about how to make money, of course—being a single mom with two children wasn't cheap.

"I'm not... I don't want weapons in my house," Raina said.

"Maybe you should get a dog," Susan said. "Like a big guard dog."

Raina looked at the twins, then nodded. "Yeah, that might be a good idea, actually. I'm more of a cat person, but a dog would be better at protecting us."

Susan finished her coffee, then put the empty cup in Raina's sink. "I should get going now, but again, welcome to the neighborhood, and remember you have my number now if you need anything. And I do mean a-n-y-t-h-i-n-g, okay? Don't hold back. Now, come here and give me a hug. You've got this; you hear me? You can do this. You are not alone."

Raina hugged Susan for a little longer than she usually would with people she had just met, but it felt so nice and comforting to know that she wasn't alone.

"Thank you," she said as she walked Susan to the door and watched her walk toward her own house across the street. She closed the door and went back to the twins, clapped her hands, and announced, "Guess what, kiddos? We're getting a dog!"

Chapter 65

THE POWERFUL HAMMERING became a part of her dream at first. It wasn't until someone yelled her name too that Meg realized someone was at the door.

"Hold on; hold on," she mumbled, still half asleep, as she tumbled out of bed and down the stairs in her PJs. "I'm coming."

"MEG!" the voice yelled, and the hammering continued. "Open up!"

Meg peeked out the window first, then opened the door.

"Trevor? What... it's seven in the morning?"

He stormed past her into the house, and she closed the door behind him. "I don't care what time it is," he said.

"What's going on?" she asked. "Did something happen?"

"Why did you do it?"

He was panting heavily now, his hair tousled.

"Why did I do what?"

He groaned. "Tell the police about the knife? Why did you do that? Now, they think I killed that girl."

He was spitting when he talked and gesticulating wildly, so Meg stepped back with a slight gasp.

"What?" he said, his face red in patches. "Are you afraid of me or something? I'm your boyfriend, Meg."

"But... you had the knife, and... you seemed so fascinated by the murder," she said. "I guess I just...."

"You just what?" he interrupted her. "Thought I might have killed her? I didn't even know her."

"What does that have to do with it?" she asked. "Maybe you thought she was me, and you really wanted to kill me."

His hands shot up to his head. "Are you insane?"

She looked down at her feet. "I'd like you to leave now. You're making me very uncomfortable."

"Oh, am I? Huh? Well, how's this for uncomfortable?" he said, then pulled out the knife from his belt.

Meg gasped and stepped back. "That's the knife from your truck. The one that was on the seat."

"Yes, I still have it," he said, waving it in front of her face. "I told the police I got rid of it, but guess what? I didn't."

"Trevor, now, take it easy, okay?" she said, taking another step back, holding out her hands in front of her as if they could somehow offer her protection from the knife or stop him from hurting her. "Don't do anything you might regret later. Let's just talk, okay?"

He grinned and took another step toward her, swinging the knife in his hands like it was just a toy.

"Does this make you nervous, huh?"

"Yes, that makes me very nervous," she said. "Please, stop it, Trevor, please."

"Do you think I'm a killer, huh?"

She shook her head. "I... I don't know. I just told the police about the knife because it made me suspicious, okay? It scared me that you had it."

He stepped forward so fast that Meg jumped. Then he laughed and poked the knife at her, pretending to be stabbing her.

"Does this scare you, huh? Does it?"

Meg could barely breathe. She fell to her knees, holding her hands above her head. "Yes, Trevor, it scares me. Please stop it."

Chapter 66

"SUSAN KELLAM IS IN THE HOSPITAL."

I had just arrived at the police station and sat down at my desk when Matt came over to me. I looked up from my computer screen.

"Really? Let's go talk to her then."

Matt shook his head and sipped his morning coffee. "Not so fast. The doctor said he had to give her a sedative earlier because she became distraught and that she is not in a condition to be interrogated yet. She is getting a psych evaluation later on, apparently. And she needs rest to recover. He will call us to let us know when we can see her."

"What happened?" I asked, relieved to know that she was being taken care of. "How did she end up in the hospital? Is she okay?"

"Well, they treated her stab wounds; one of them had sprung open, and she had lost some blood, and then she was apparently hit by a car and broke both her legs. She is not in good shape, but she is stable."

I leaned back in my chair with a deep sigh. The poor woman had been through so much.

"Oh, good. Has anyone notified her daughter?"

"Not yet."

"Okay," I said. "I'll go tell Meg that we found her mother and tell her what happened to her. She needs to know."

"You want me to go with you?" Matt asked. "I have some time."

I paused. He noticed.

"Oh, you're bringing Alex; never mind then."

"No," I said. "He's working on something else this morning, some article he is writing, and he's not joining me till later."

Matt smiled. "Okay, then, I'll go with you. Just let me finish up what I was working on, and then we'll go."

Half an hour later, we were driving toward Snug Harbor in Matt's police cruiser. I had an uneasy sensation in my body that I couldn't get rid of. I was worried, and I didn't know why.

"Why are you biting your nails?" Matt asked as he drove up her street. "You only do that when you're nervous."

"I don't know," I said and forced myself to stop. It was a terrible habit, and my nails were suffering from it. They looked awful. "I just don't have a good feeling about this, but I have no idea why."

He parked the cruiser in the driveway, and we got out. I touched my gun lightly, as I always did when anxious about going into a situation. Matt saw it but didn't comment. I was making him nervous, too; I could tell.

I rang the doorbell, but nothing happened.

Then, I knocked.

"Meg?"

Still, nothing. As I knocked again, the front door slid open. I looked at Matt. He pushed it completely open, then yelled.

"Hello? Meg Kellam? This is the police. Is anyone home?"

I looked around the house's foyer, then noticed a vase had been knocked down from the table next to the door. A picture frame was shattered and lying on the tiles.

I pulled out my gun.

"I'm going in; call for backup."

Chapter 67

"TREVOR, WHERE ARE WE GOING?"

He didn't answer. Meg looked out the window of his truck and at the neighborhood flying by.

"Trevor?"

"What?"

"Where are you taking me?"

"I just thought we could go for a little drive," he said.

Meg looked at his hand. He was still holding the knife in it. She wondered if she could somehow snatch it from his grip, but she wasn't sure she dared to.

"Why are you being like this?" she asked. "I'm sorry for talking to the police and telling them you have a knife."

He didn't say anything, but he hit the accelerator, and the truck roared. Meg stared at the knife.

Then, her phone rang. It was in her pocket, and she pulled it out and looked at the display. Trevor had let her get dressed before he told her to get in the truck. He had knocked over some things at the house when trying to grab her. He was really angry.

"Don't answer it," he hissed.

"But... what if it's important?"

"Just ignore it."

She stared at the ringing phone. She wanted to press the button and take it, then scream that she had been kidnapped and for whoever it was on the other end to call nine-one-one.

But she didn't dare.

She put it back in her pocket as it continued to ring. It stopped for a few seconds but then started to ring again.

"It must be important," she said. "If they keep calling."

"Who is it?"

"I don't recognize the number."

"Then, don't take it," he said. "Just ignore them. And shut off the ringer. Who has sound on their phone these days anyway?"

She did as he told her, then put it back in her pocket. She felt it vibrate again, and it was driving her nuts.

"Where are we going, Trevor?" she tried again.

He drove faster and swung the truck around a car, moving into the opposite lane. A car coming toward them honked loudly, and Meg shrieked.

"Stop it, Trevor; do you hear me? You're gonna kill us both."

"No, I'm mad at you. I don't want to talk to you."

"Then just stop the truck on the side of the road and let me get out," she said, her voice almost breaking. "Please?"

"No."

"Come on, Trevor," she said. "It's me. You love me, remember? You don't want to hurt me."

"I still can't believe you would do that—that you would rat me out like that. I mean, who are you even? I didn't think you would ever betray me."

"It's me, Trevor. I'm still me. Please, just slow down."

He didn't. He almost ran into a large truck as he passed another car. Meg felt her heart knock against her rib cage. He turned the truck into his lane just in time while the truck honked.

Then, Meg thought of something. She put her hand on his arm and started to caress it.

"Trevor?"

He didn't look at her. His knuckles holding the wheel were turning white.

Then, she let her hand slide down to his thigh and started to caress him there. Finally, he paid attention.

"You know what we haven't done in a long time?"

"I'm listening."

"How about you take us down to the lake by the next exit and stop the car there. I will give you whatever you want."

"Whatever I want? Even the thing you never want to do?"

She smiled, then nodded, licking her lips. "Of course. Consider it a make-up gift. A way for me to really show you just how sorry I am."

Chapter 68

I PRESSED the call button again and waited. Matt looked at me anxiously as I hung up and shook my head.

"She's not picking up."

"She's not in the house or the yard," Matt said. "Her car is in the garage next to her mom's."

"I don't like this," I said, biting my lip and looking around the living room where we were standing. Two patrol cars had come as our back-up and were helping out searching for Meg. One of the officers, Officer Craig, came up toward us.

"I spoke to one of the neighbors," he said. "A guy who lives two houses down the street. He said he saw a truck in the driveway earlier this morning. He says it's the same truck he sees there a lot and that it belongs to that McCoy kid."

"Trevor," I said and looked at Matt. "The boyfriend."

Matt lifted his eyebrows. "She did tell us he had that knife."

"Let's put out a search for both him and her and the truck. I don't like the way this feels or the look of that vase and the shattered picture. It looks like there was a struggle, which makes me scared for her safety."

Matt nodded. "I'll make it happen right away."

He left me, and I sat down heavily on one of the chairs in the living room. I couldn't stop being angry with myself. I had spoken to Trevor; I had him. I could have done more.

I stared at the bookshelves surrounding the fireplace in the living room, then got up and looked at the books up close. Some of them had been taken out recently and put back in again but not pushed all the way in to fit with the others in a straight line. It was strange because all of them were written by the same person.

I pulled one out and flipped through it, then grabbed another and read the back cover.

"Done," Matt said, coming up behind me. "What's that?"

"Have you ever heard of a Dr. Milton?"

Matt shook his head. "Can't say I have."

"I know who he is."

I looked up and spotted Alex standing at the entrance to the living room. "I hope you don't mind me coming here," he said and stepped closer. "I was done with my article and wanted to find you. They told me you were here. I had a feeling you were doing police work without me there to record it."

"Not him again," Matt said.

"What do you know of him?" I asked, ignoring Matt's childish outburst. He acted like we were back in high school, and it was frankly getting a little old. "What do you know about Dr. Milton?"

"If it's the same one, I interviewed him some years ago," Alex said. "He's a prominent psychiatrist. He's written a ton of books on the study of twins. He's quite radical."

"In what way?"

"He created the *Evil Twin theory*. Or rather, it's been known forever throughout history, but he spent his life trying to prove that the mythology surrounding especially identical twins is true. There is a 'good one' and therefore must be a 'bad one.' Like Yin and Yang, black and white, opposites must co-exist like dueling forces. He genuinely believed that if a set of twins were born, one would be good and the other evil—that their upbringing and socialization had nothing to do with it. No matter what happened to them, one of them would remain bad."

"That sounds quite extreme," Matt said.

"You and I can agree on that; nevertheless, Dr. Milton dedicated his entire career and life to proving his theory."

I glared at Alex. "You keep talking about him like he is dead?"

Alex nodded. He grabbed his phone and showed me an article. "He died a few weeks ago. He was stabbed to death in his own home in Colorado. His wife and kids found him in his study."

I skimmed through the article, then looked up at Alex, a million thoughts rushing through my mind at once. Something here didn't add up—a lot, in fact.

At that exact second, my phone rang. I picked it up and walked away from the others to talk.

It was Dr. Mendez, the ME.

"I have tried to figure this out for so long, and now finally I have," she said. "You won't believe what I have to tell you."

Chapter 69

THEN:

Duke was such a pleasure to have around and soon became a big part of the family. The thirty-inch tall, long-legged Great Dane weighed more than Raina did and looked vicious to anyone who didn't know him but was, in fact, the gentlest giant on the planet. He would play with the children in the yard and let them crawl all over him, but he would bark at night if anyone approached the house, even though Raina knew he just wanted to play with whoever was there. Anyone who didn't know him would think otherwise, and in that sense, he managed to make her feel safer in her new home.

The other ladies in the neighborhood became her friends quickly, and she felt welcome there; soon, they all seemed to be settled in. She didn't think much about Tom or if he was looking for her or not and soon became so busy with her job at a local clothing store that she almost forgot she had a life before she got there. The kids seemed to thrive, even though they had to spend hours in daycare every day. Well, at least Charlotte did. Noah came home almost every day with a note from his teachers telling Raina about his inappropriate behavior, biting someone, or not following the rules. He was a handful, but then again, he was a boy, and it was only natural that he was a little rowdier than Charlotte, who was always so gentle and sweet.

"Wait until they become teenagers," her neighbor from across the street, Susan, told her. "Then it will switch around on you, and she will be the impossible one while he will be the good kid. Just wait and see."

Raina so hoped she was right. She had to admit there were days when she resented the boy so much that it made her feel sick. What kind of a mother thought that way about her own son?

One afternoon, she was sitting out on the back porch, watching the kids play in the backyard. It was one of those fall afternoons when it was still just warm enough to sit outside, but you knew that it would quickly grow very cold as soon as the sun set behind the trees in the neighboring yard. She was enjoying her hot tea, wishing the summer would have lasted longer. She hated the long winters that would drag out for months and ached to live in a place that had summer all year long. The twins had turned three and were beginning to talk a lot. Most of it was gibberish, but Raina understood what they meant, as a good mom often does.

When Charlotte came running up to her, showing her a bug she had found on the ground, she understood that she was saying:

"Isn't it pretty?"

Even though no one else would have gotten that from the sounds coming out of her cute little mouth, Raina did.

"It is very pretty," Raina said and stared at the black beetle that made her skin crawl. She kissed her daughter's forehead, and Charlotte giggled happily, then pranced back into the yard that was so magical to her.

For a second, Raina wished she would always stay this way—so enchanted by everything she encountered along her way. Meanwhile, she looked for Noah and saw him push the dog to the side as he was in his way. Duke moved lazily, and Noah grinned as he lifted his fist and hit the dog right on the snout.

"Noah," Raina said. "Be nice to Duke. He's our friend."

She got up, then went to the dog and petted him. "Do like this, sweetie. Nice and gentle."

Noah looked up at his mom, then grinned. He petted the dog like she showed him, then pulled Duke's ear hard.

"No, Noah," Raina said and pulled him away from the dog. "Be nice to him."

Noah pulled out of her grip, then stormed away, back to the playhouse in the back of the yard. Raina shook her head and went inside to get Duke a treat for being so patient with the kids. He truly was a good dog. Most dogs would have snapped at the kid when he pulled the ear like that or punched him. But Duke was so gentle. He knew the children were fragile and that he had to take care of them; Raina was sure of that. He would never harm either of the children. He understood a lot more than they thought he did. She had grown to love the dog more than she ever imagined she would.

Raina walked outside on the porch, closed the door behind her, and called for the dog to come.

"Duke, come get your treat, buddy. Come."

When the dog didn't come, Raina walked down the stairs and into the yard. She could hear Charlotte gibbering away by the roses and see her curly head poke up between them. But where was Noah? And where was Duke?

"Duke? Come here, boy. Come."

As she approached the playhouse, she heard a strange sound.

Tap-Tap-Tap

Raina felt uneasy and rushed around to the playhouse entrance, then peeked inside.

"Noah? Duke?"

They weren't in there. Then she heard the sound again.

Tap-Tap-Tap

"What is that?" she mumbled. "Where is it coming from?"

She turned around to the sound of it, then felt her heart drop.

"The well, the dried-up well!"

She hurried through the bushes in the back and spotted the area with the well that still hadn't been covered up, even though she had told the landlord a million times that he needed to do it. Susan had helped Raina put some wood on top of it so that no one could fall in, but it was only there loosely.

"Noah?"

She approached the area and spotted Noah sitting there, squatting next to the well, looking inside it. The wood had been pushed aside, and the well was open. Noah was tapping on the wood while laughing.

"Duke, Du-u-uke," he called, sounding like he was mocking him, and that's when she realized it.

Duke is in the well. Duke has fallen in the well!

She rushed closer, then grabbed Noah by his arm and pulled him away. She peeked into the well and spotted Duke at the very bottom. Her heart then dropped—the dog was alive. He was moving down there but whimpering in pain from what appeared to be at least one broken leg caused by the fall.

Sweat sprang to her forehead as she thought about what to do.

"How are we going to get him out of there?" she asked.

She looked at Noah, who stared down at the dog, giggling as only a three-year-old could. Then, she paused.

"How did the wood get pushed to the side?" she asked. She looked at the boy. "Noah? Noah? What did you do? Look at me, boy. Did you push the dog into the well? Noah?"

He looked up at her, then tilted his head. He shook it.

"No."

"I think you did. Oh, my God, what are we going to do? Noah, why would you push Duke into the well? WHY, Noah?"

He looked straight into her eyes, then said in the same gibberish that only Raina could decipher, "I don't like him."

Chapter 70

TREVOR PULLED the wheel and took the exit. They bumped into a small road toward the big lake and found a spot in the shade between the tall trees with the Spanish moss hanging from the branches. The lake was so quiet, the water barely moving. A grey heron was fishing by the shore, walking stoically on its long, thin legs, cautiously moving forward, careful not to stir the waters and scare away any fish or alert the gators of its presence.

Trevor put the truck in park but left the engine on for the AC. It was boiling hot outside.

He smiled. "You sure?"

She nodded. "Yeah, I want to. I really am sorry for what I did. I don't know what came over me. I know you. Of course, you didn't kill my sister. I got caught up in the tension and everyone accusing everyone. I want to make it up to you. I truly do. I want you to realize that I mean it."

He scoffed, still smiling. "It was kind of crazy when the police came to my house and everything. I couldn't believe it."

She wrinkled her nose. "I'm sorry."

He nodded. She moved closer and let her hand slide up toward his crotch. She touched him, and he moaned.

"I will make you feel really good if you'll let me."

She gave him a pleading look.

"Will you?"

"Oh, I'll let you, all right," he said, then opened his pants.

She closed her eyes and touched it, then whispered. "You might want to put down that knife. It kind of spoils the mood."

"Of course," he said and dropped the knife to the floor. She watched it land, then returned her focus to him. She took his head between her hands and kissed him while rubbing his crotch.

"Oh, God, I have missed this," he moaned between kisses.

She bent over his lap. He closed his eyes and leaned his head back.

"Oh, yes."

While his eyes were closed, she reached down her hand and grabbed the knife while moaning and rubbing him.

He didn't see it. He was lost in his pleasure, even when he opened his eyes again.

"I want to be with you; can I? You know... the way we talked about?"

She smiled while hiding the hand holding the knife.

"Sure. But be gentle."

"Always am, baby, always am."

She took his hand, and he slid it up her pants. He opened her pants and put his hand into her panties. He pulled his hand out fast. Their eyes met as his shot open in terror.

"Wh... what... what the heck?"

Then she laughed, all while lifting the knife and piercing it through his chest. She pulled it out and stabbed it into his abdomen. Blood ran from his mouth and dripped onto her legs.

"You're... you're... a...."

She pulled out the knife again, then stabbed it into his throat, closing her eyes in pleasure as she listened to it penetrate the aorta. Then, as he slowly died, she whispered, "Yes, my dear. That I am."

She waited until he didn't move anymore, then dragged him out and placed him on the ground. She dragged him across the ground and put him in the river, pushing him into the middle of the lake.

She stood for a few minutes, waiting for the gators to find him, then smiled widely as she watched them tear his body to shreds.

When the spectacle was over, she got into the truck and drove away, foot flooring the accelerator, while mumbling to herself, "It's not like I liked him very much."

Chapter 71

"WHAT IS SHE DOING? She's been sitting there for the past fifteen minutes, reading?" Alex asked.

"Shh. Let her work her magic," Matt said. "Don't disturb her."

I didn't look up from the book I was skimming through. I didn't pay any attention to the two of them at all. Pieces of the puzzle were falling into place as I turned the pages one after another, my fingers moving fast, my eyes speed-reading across the pages.

I couldn't believe what I was learning.

Finally, I closed the book. They both looked at me.

"What?" Alex said, throwing out his arms. "What's going on?"

I glanced at them without really looking directly at either of them. My mind was wandering.

"What was that phone call you got?" Matt asked.

I bit the side of my cheek while letting the pieces settle in place. I didn't have all of them, but a picture was emerging from them anyway. And it certainly wasn't a pretty one.

"Eva Rae?" Alex asked. "Can you tell us anything?"

I exhaled, then got up from the chair, the book still in my hand.

I handed it to Matt. "This is evidence. Make sure it is secured properly. It could prove to be very vital for the trial later on."

"Okay?" he asked. "And?"

I nodded, then looked directly at him. He looked confused.

"And then we go to the hospital."

I grabbed my purse and started to walk toward the front door.

"Why are we going to the hospital?" Matt asked.

"We need to have a talk with Susan Kellam," I said. "She's got some serious explaining to do."

"But the doctor said she was in no condition to talk to us yet," Matt said, hurrying up behind me as I stormed toward the cruiser.

"I don't care," I said, walking with long determined steps. "I will wait there until she is ready if I have to."

"But...?"

I ignored him and continued. I got into the car and slammed the door.

Alex came out too, hurried to the cruiser, and then jumped in the back. I took the wheel while Matt was in the passenger seat. I started the engine and backed out of the driveway.

"Care to at least explain what you read in the book?" Matt asked. "You're kind of leaving us in the dark a little here."

"I will tell you everything," I said and stepped on the accelerator, then put the siren on, riding through the quiet neighborhood with all the expensive houses right on the water.

"But not now. If I'm right about what I think this is, then there's no time. We can't waste another minute."

Chapter 72

I CAN'T JUST LIE HERE *and wait for death to find me.*

Susan could literally hear her own heartbeat as it hammered in her chest. She couldn't stand just lying there, unable to move while she waited.

Waited for what?

"I need to get up," she said and looked at the nurse sitting in the chair leaning against the wall. She was reading some romance book and had been engrossed in it for hours on end. Susan couldn't stand the sight of her anymore. She was under observation because they believed she was suicidal. Yes, she got that; thank you very much, but this nurse wasn't even looking at her.

And what difference did it make if she killed herself or someone else did it?

"Please, stay in bed, Mrs. Kellam," the nurse said, not even looking up from her darn book. She turned a page. "It's for your own good."

"But I can't stay here any longer. Can't you just put me in a wheelchair or something?"

The nurse looked at her from over the rim of her glasses. "You know why we need to keep you here under observation."

"If I promise not to hurt myself?"

She smiled. It came off as slightly condescending. "We can't do that, I'm afraid. Only a few more hours, and then it's over."

"What's the difference of a few hours?" Susan asked.

The nurse scoffed.

"Doctor's orders," she chirped, and her eyes returned to the book.

Susan leaned back on her pillow, feeling uneasy, telling herself she could make it. Just a few more hours.

But I'm still not going to be able to run if I need to, to get away.

She stared at both her legs—one fractured thigh and one fractured ankle. Plus, all the stab wounds in her chest and back. She was in an awful state. Actually, it was quite a miracle that she was still alive.

But for how long?

She tried to sit up. The nurse exhaled. "Please, ma'am, you can't get up, at least not yet. I can't...."

She was interrupted when someone walked through the door of the hospital room. Startled at this, the nurse stood to her feet.

"Really, sir, you're not allowed in here. This patient is...."

The hooded man smiled, grabbed a chair, and slammed it into the nurse, knocking her to the ground. Susan watched her go down; her lips were quivering as she realized she wasn't coming back up. Then she looked at the man in front of her.

"So, this is where you're hiding," he said.

"Get away from me," she said.

That made him smile. "Or what? What are you going to do?"

"W-what do you want?"

"What do I want? Hm," he said. "Let me just think about that one for a second. Oh, yeah, I want you to pay for what you've done."

"I lost my daughter. She was my everything," she hissed. "Isn't that enough punishment?"

"Hm, I guess I should know the answer to that one, huh? Oh, wait, I do."

He looked at her, coming closer, then grabbed a pillow from the bed next to hers. He approached her with it, coming closer to her face, then peeked behind it and said:

"No."

He covered her face with the pillow and held it tight.

Chapter 73

THE ELEVATOR WAS TOO SLOW. It felt like it took an eternity for it to reach the hospital's third floor. I had called for back-up and told the security guards to put the hospital in lockdown.

Now, I was standing with Matt and Alex in this small metal box, waiting for it to make its way to the floor that Susan Kellam was on, and it felt like it was going backward. Or at least like we were barely moving.

"Come on; come on," I said.

Finally, it dinged, and the doors opened. I grabbed my gun from my holster and pulled it out. I walked down the hallway, holding it ready. The alarm sounded, and panic was visible on the nurses' faces. Matt told them to take cover somewhere safe. A doctor protested. He was yelling something at me, but I ignored him and showed him my badge while rushing past him.

The woman at the front desk had told us that Susan was in room 318, and I hurried down the hallway, then found the room near the end. I stopped. Matt was right behind me. Alex was keeping his distance as I had told him to. I had said that coming with us was at his own risk. He assured me he would be fine and not get himself in danger, that he was used to dangerous situations as a war reporter, and this was nothing. Then he said there were plenty of other civilians present at the hospital, and we couldn't stop him from being there, even if we told him not to come.

"What are we looking at here?" Matt asked. "What do you expect to find behind that door?"

I held my gun tight, then locked eyes with him for a second. "Our killer."

I grabbed the door handle, then pushed the door open. Inside, I saw someone hunched over the person in the bed, a pillow on top of her face, the person straining to hold it down.

"Stop it right there," I said, pointing my gun at him.

He didn't let go but kept pressing on Susan's face. She was moving but only sporadically, like spasms. On the floor lay a young nurse, bleeding from her head.

"STOP what you're doing, or I will shoot," I said. I walked closer, aiming the gun directly at him.

The man looked at us with his hair tousled and his face red. Then he lifted the pillow from her face and threw it on the floor with a deep exhale. Matt walked up to him and pulled him to the side while I ran to Susan, feeling her throat for a pulse.

"Susan? Susan? Can you hear me?"

But there was no response and no pulse. "I need help in here!"

Several nurses came running in, and they started giving Susan CPR, then brought in the defibrillator.

I walked to the man that Matt had put in handcuffs. "There's a special place in hell for people like you. Trying to kill your own mother!"

Matt looked at me, then at the guy. "Meg?"

"That's not Meg," I said. "That's Meg's twin."

"I'm confused," Matt said. "I thought the twin was the girl in the pool?"

I was breathing heavily in distress and anger. "No. I'm afraid that the girl we pulled out of the pool was Meg."

I heard the nurses cheer as Susan's heartbeat came back. I breathed, more relieved as they told us she was back and stable for now.

"Susan knew it from the moment we pulled her out of there," I said. "That's why she had to run."

Matt ran a hand through his hair, staring at me, baffled. "So... you're telling me this guy is Meg's twin?"

I nodded. "Yes. He was born a boy but has been raised a girl. It was my oldest child who made me realize what is actually possible today. With hormone treatment early on in life, he never went through puberty as a boy, and since he was pumped with estrogen, he developed breasts and feminine traits. But he was born a boy, which made it easy for him to take his sister's place once he killed her. It was Dr. Mendez that called me earlier, and she told me she had finally figured it out. See, she didn't understand how identical twins could have different sexes. I didn't know they were different sexes until then. Usually, identical twins are always of the same sex, but it has been known to deviate under rare circumstances. It's called *sesquizygotic* twins and is extremely rare."

Matt looked even more confused. "But... but why would he kill her?"

Chapter 74

THEN:

Raina knew she couldn't take her eyes off her little boy. And it wasn't for the reasons it had been when they were younger, and she was scared he and his sister would be kidnapped. No, this was much worse. After Duke ended up dying in the well because they couldn't get him up, Raina feared her little boy more than anything. She worried about what he was capable of and couldn't stop thinking about Tom and the twin sister his mother said he had killed.

Was she telling the truth?

And did he end up killing her as well? His own mother? To keep her quiet?

The thought made her shiver in her bed at night when she lay awake, wondering what to do. She had seen the evil in Noah from the beginning but always made up excuses for him.

He's just a boy—they're different, rowdier, more violent. It's normal. He'll grow out of it.

But since Duke died, there were no more excuses to be made.

Raina shared her worries with her neighbor, Susan, when she visited, and she no longer sugar-coated it. She told her flat out that she was terrified of the boy.

"What if he kills me in my sleep?" she asked.

Susan understood her concerns and wanted to help. A few weeks after the incident with Duke, she brought Susan a book.

"Here. Read this. It's by Dr. Milton, who is a prominent psychiatrist. He has some interesting theories on twins and their nature. I think you should read it."

So, Raina did. One Saturday afternoon, she let the children play in the backyard, and she sat down with her coffee and started to read. The book had her from the first line, and she couldn't put it down. Everything this guy wrote about twins could have been taken from her own life.

She couldn't believe it. Suddenly, it actually made sense.

Raina kept reading for hours and forgot about her children and to keep an eye on them for some time, and it wasn't until everything suddenly grew very quiet in the yard that she noticed something was off.

Where are the kids?

She put the book down anxiously, then walked toward the end of the yard, taking each step faster and faster to get there.

The well. The darn well!

"Noah? Charlotte?"

Her voice was trembling, her legs shivering beneath her as she started to run.

"NOAH? CHARLOTTE?"

She rushed through the bushes and found the site of the well. There, she saw them, but she thought it had to be an illusion.

What are they doing?

Charlotte was on the ground, on her back, while Noah was on top of her, his small hands wrapped around her skinny neck.

It took Raina a few seconds to realize what was really happening.

He's strangling her!

Raina rushed toward them, screaming his name at the top of her lungs.

"NOAH! Let her GO! STOP!"

But he didn't react. He kept strangling the little girl, and she was turning blue as Raina reached them. She screamed in panic, then grabbed the little boy by the shoulders and pulled him off his sister. He yelled in anger and fought her, his fists hitting her face and abdomen. She pushed him away, then rushed to attend to Charlotte.

"Charlotte, baby? Are you okay?"

The girl coughed and was getting color in her cheeks again. Raina took her in her arms, then rocked her back and forth.

"Oh, sweet baby, I thought I had lost you. I'm so sorry I didn't keep an eye on you both; I will never let you out of my sight again."

She looked at her boy, who was standing by the edge of the well. He was staring at them, then laughing almost manically like he thought this was just a game. Seeing this, Raina lost it. She let go of her daughter, then walked to him and gave him a push—not a very hard one, but just enough.

As he stumbled back, their eyes met right at the very second his little body started to fall.

Raina held her breath as he disappeared into the darkness. It took a few seconds before she heard the bump, then he started to cry.

"Mommy? Mommy? Help?"

Raina looked down at him in the darkness.

"I'll get you help; don't worry," she said.

Noah was crying now, and Raina grabbed her cell phone, then

walked toward Charlotte and held her hand tight in hers, fighting not to break down in tears.

"Hello? Yes, this is Raina Hudson. I need to talk to Dr. Milton, please. Tell him it's urgent, please."

Chapter 75

"IT WAS AN EXPERIMENT."

Matt gave me a look, shaking his head. "What do you mean? What kind of experiment?"

"Dr. Milton writes about them in his book—the one I gave you. His theory was to prove that even if twins were separated early in life and raised completely differently, even as a different gender, there would always be a good one and a bad one. It was inevitable. That was why he always looked for families with twins who were willing to help him in his experiments, and that's where Susan came in. They have different names in the book, but I recognized them immediately. Susan was terrified of her own son, and that's why she asked Dr. Milton for help. She believed in his theories. He forged the birth certificate and the birth records, so it says that Susan only had one child. I recognized his name, and that's when I realized what had been going on."

"You must understand. I'm not a bad person. I'm really not. But I couldn't live in fear for the rest of my life," Susan said.

She had opened her eyes and looked at us, tears welling up in them. "I didn't know what to do. I took my baby girl, Charlotte was her name back then, with me and took my neighbor's name, then changed hers as well to Meghan. I didn't want anything to do with our past. I wanted to start over completely fresh. So, we moved to Florida with new names and a new birth certificate for Meg. I was now Susan Kellam. We were doing great until this happened—until Noah found us." She looked at her son. He was standing with his head bowed. "I knew it the moment they pulled Meg out of the pool. I knew it was you who had come back. I just knew it was you. You sick bastard."

"You're the one who is sick," he said.

"I'm your mother. You just tried to kill me—smothering me with a freaking pillow. That's sick. You murdered your sister."

"You don't get to call yourself my mom. Moms don't leave their sons. They don't push them into a well and then give them to some doctor to experiment on them. How do you think it made me feel when I read the diaries and his reports? I read all of them, and that's when I realized what was going on. He came to visit me at the house of the family he had placed me with, once a month for all of my upbringing, and I always thought he was from the city or DCF, but he would give me a physical, and he would speak to me and show me pictures of killings, blood, and such. He would ask me how they made me feel. He wanted to see if they could get the evil out of me. That's what the report said. That if I was raised with a completely different family and even as a girl, then how would that change me? One day, after his visit, I followed him home to his house and broke in when no one was home. I read it all—everything he had written about me and the other twins he experimented on. He called it the *Evil Twin Theory*. He claims to have proven that one twin will always be evil. That's his scientific proof—me. I burned down the house I lived in, then took off, looking for my sister. I found everything I needed on her and my mom and dad in his papers. I never found my dad, but mom was pretty easy, especially since Dr. Milton followed my sister's progress to compare us. So, I found the address and new names and came here. I observed them for a while and realized I wanted to destroy them, take the life back that should have been mine. I took her place."

"You mean you killed her," I said.

"She was having a party, and in the morning, when everyone was asleep, she walked outside to the pool and started to clean up. I snuck up on her, then stabbed her and let her fall into the water."

"Why didn't you remove her body? If you wanted to take her place?" I asked.

"Because I wanted our mother to realize what was happening. I wanted her to suffer from knowing her daughter was dead and that I was coming for her. I wanted to see her in pain. And I knew she could never tell anyone what was going on because that meant she'd have to tell people what she had done."

"And she did spend an awful lot of energy trying to hide that," a voice coming from the doorway said.

I turned to look and spotted Alex standing there. He wasn't alone. Someone was holding a gun to his head.

Chapter 76

"SEAN ANDERSSON?"

He stared at me, nostrils flaring. I couldn't stop looking at the finger on the trigger of the gun. Alex looked terrified.

"Let go of my son."

He nodded toward Noah, then added, "Take off the cuffs, or this guy is gone. And place your guns on the floor, then kick them over here."

I nodded to Matt and signaled for him to obey. I took out my gun, kicked it toward him, and held both hands in the air. Matt did the same, then opened the cuffs. Noah stared at his father while Sean signaled for him to come closer. Noah walked up to him, and Sean smiled.

"My son. My handsome boy. You have no idea how long I have been looking for you."

"Tom, please don't hurt anyone," Susan said from the bed. "Please, put down the gun. It's all my fault. Please."

"You're darn right that it's all your fault," Tom snapped and pointed the gun at her. It was shaking in his hand. That's how agitated he was. He was a dangerous man. "I ought to kill you right here."

Susan hid her face between her hands and sobbed. "I'm so sorry. I truly am. I'm so, so sorry."

"You stole my children from me. Why, Raina? Why?"

"I was scared, Tom. You had that bloody shirt. I… you killed your own mother? And your sister?"

"Tom," I said, stepping forward. "There's no need for anyone else to get hurt. We understand that you have been through a lot, but please think about your…."

He pointed the gun at me, and I stopped talking. I broke into an instant sweat, feeling how it rolled down the sides of my face.

"Shut up," he said. "Just shut up."

He stood for a second, gun shaking in his hand.

"What do you want?" I asked.

"I want the doors opened to this hospital, so my son and I can leave," he said. "I want the choppers outside called off, and no one shoots when we walk out."

"Okay, but you must let Alex go," I said.

"No fricking way," he said. "He comes with us."

My eyes met Alex's, and I saw how terrified he was. I was scared too.

"All right," I said.

I signaled for Matt to give them the order.

"Stand back," he said into his radio. "All units stand down. Target is coming out, and he has a hostage."

Alex protested. "E-Eva Rae?"

I stepped forward. "I need to have the assurance that you won't hurt him. And then I need to know how we'll get him back. Unharmed."

Tom smiled. "We'll make sure you find him. We're going to leave now, and no one moves in this room or outside. Do you hear me?"

"Take me instead," I said. "He's just a reporter. He's nothing."

Now, it was Matt's turn to protest. "No. Eva Rae. Think of your children."

"Nice try," Tom said. "But we'll stick to this guy. Move back and don't move a muscle in the next ten minutes."

Then they pulled out of the room and disappeared, closing the door behind them.

Chapter 77

IT WAS the longest ten minutes of my entire life. I stared at the clock on the wall, and it felt like it was going backward. Meanwhile, Matt was on my case about Alex.

"You had to bring him, didn't you? I knew this was going to happen. I just knew it. That's why we don't bring civilians on assignments."

He was right. It was my decision to let him come with us, and I was mad at myself for letting this happen. I should never have brought him. If he were killed, it would be all my fault. I had just never thought this would happen. But that's the thing; you never do, right?

Not until it's too late.

I kept my eyes on the stupid clock, willing it to go faster.

Come on. Come on.

Five, seven, and finally, ten minutes had passed. I grabbed my gun from the floor, where Tom had left them, then stormed out the door, Matt right behind me. We took the stairs down two steps at a time, then ran into the parking lot, where the chief was waiting for us.

"We did as you told us. We let them go. All three."

"Where did they go?"

"We do, of course, have a tail on him and cars on every street corner," Annie said. "Keeping an eye on him. They saw him drive toward the cape."

"He's going for the marina. He probably has a boat out there," I said when my phone vibrated in my pocket. I picked it up. The display showed No Caller ID.

"Hello?"

"Agent Thomas," the voice said. "The ten minutes are up."

"Let him go," I said. "Alex didn't do anything wrong. And you promised you wouldn't harm him."

"Oh, I won't," he said. "But my son might. Goodbye."

He hung up. I groaned loudly and stared at the phone in my hand.

"Can we trace it?" I asked.

"We might," Annie said. "But it will take some time."

"I fear we don't have that. Alex will be dead if we take too long."

"Our tail lost him," someone said to Annie. "Up by 520."

"Do we have any choppers nearby?"

"No choppers," I said. "If he hears the sound of it, he'll kill Alex."

"Then what do you want me to do here?" Annie said.

Think, Eva Rae. Where could they go? Think.

"You've closed down all the bridges, right?" I asked.

She nodded. "Yes. They can't get to the mainland."

"At least not by car," I said.

I thought about Tom, who was Sean when I met him. Sean, who lived in the mountains, in a ski area. Sean who....

"Jet ski," I said.

"What's that?" Matt asked.

254

"Last time I chased him, when I lost him on the mountainside, he was riding a snowmobile."

"The closest jet ski rental place is on 520," Matt said. "By Banana River."

"Let's go, people," Annie said and clapped her hands. She signaled for her men to get in their cars. "We need to get boats in the water."

I stopped her. "I think Matt and I need to go alone. If this guy hears us all coming, he will kill Alex. This is important. I can't lose him."

"Okay," Annie said, then went to the back of her car and pulled out two Kevlar vests. "But at least wear these. I'm not losing my two best people on the same day."

Chapter 78

I THREW the car into the gravel outside the small yellow building. The guy working there came out.

"Hey, do you have reservations? Because we are fully booked for the entire day."

I showed him my badge. He backed up.

"Whoa, man."

"I need to ask you a few questions. Have you recently rented out jet skis to three men?"

"Yeah, they just left a while ago. They rented two jet skis, the last ones I had available. They took off toward Ski Island."

"I'm gonna need a jet ski."

"Hey," he said. "I just told you that I don't have any available. Don't the police have their own?"

"We do," Matt said. "But it'll take too long to get them here. So, we need yours. Now."

He raised his hands. "Okay, man. There's one left that isn't out there already, but it's reserved for someone at two o'clock."

We rushed to the dock, then found the jet ski he was talking about and jumped on it. I turned it on, and Matt sat in the back, holding my waist. I took off so abruptly that he almost fell off.

"Have you ever driven one of these things?" he yelled against the wind blowing in his face.

"No," I yelled back while water sprayed our faces. "But it can't be much harder than riding a snowmobile, can it?"

"What?" Matt screamed. "Didn't you almost kill both you and Alex on that thing up there?"

I continued, speeding up and ignoring him. It didn't take me long before I spotted two jet skis in front of us, heading toward Ski Island. It was a small, deserted party island that many people went to on the weekends and drank and danced. I had been there many times as a young adult, going by boat with my friends.

Tom and Noah passed the island and continued going north. I set after them, taking the ski to its max. As we came closer, Tom spotted us when he turned his head. He had Alex with him.

"He might shoot Alex if we get any closer," Matt yelled behind me. "What is your brilliant plan here?"

I continued unabated and soon came closer. Tom saw this and looked back at me. Noah was on the other ski, following his tail. Tom swung the gun to threaten me. I smiled. Not the reaction he was going for, I guess.

"That's it, my friend," I mumbled against the wind. "Keep looking at me and not ahead."

"Eva Rae, what are you doing?"

"Using my knowledge. I know these waters; I know this area like the back of my hand. He knows the mountains; that's why he escaped the last time. But this is my turf. I grew up here and have been boating here all my life."

"So have I," Matt said, but what does that have to...?"

We looked at the two jet skis ahead of us. They both came to a sudden and very abrupt halt. Surprised by this, it sent all three bodies flying into the air. All of them landed in the water with loud splashes.

"Ah, the sandbars," Matt said.

"Yup. Some of them move, but this one has been here forever," I said and slowed down. I rode up next to Alex and pulled him out of the water. He climbed onto the back and held onto Matt's back. I rode cautiously toward the sandbar and then stopped on top of it. Matt took off his vest, then jumped into the water and set off after Noah, who was treading water. I had my eyes on Tom, who was struggling to keep his head above water.

"He can't swim," Alex said. "He told me earlier."

I took off my vest too, then handed it to Alex before I jumped into the water and swam toward him. His head bobbed underneath the surface but didn't come back up again. I swam faster. As I reached the spot where he had been, I dove under. I kept swimming down until my hands touched his. I managed to grab him by the shoulders, then pulled him up to the surface. I then swam toward the jet skis with him on my back. I pulled him up on the ski and gave him mouth to mouth. Water spurted out of him, and he coughed. I put him on the side, breathing heavily in distress.

"I called for help," Matt said. He was holding a gun to Noah's head and holding him tight so he wouldn't try to run. Alex was paler than a sheet but alive.

"Chopper will be here any minute."

Chapter 79

WE WERE all airlifted into the chopper as it arrived. Chief Annie sat inside of it and helped me get in. I was holding Tom, who kept drifting in and out of consciousness. Noah, Matt, and Alex followed. Seconds later, we were heading to the Holmes Regional Hospital that had a landing platform on the roof.

"Come on, Tom; hold on for me," I said.

Tom had turned purple and wouldn't wake up. I gave him mouth to mouth again. It woke him up. He looked at me, then grabbed my collar and pulled me close. It was hard to hear over the sounds of the chopper, but I still managed to understand what he said, "I just wanted my children back. I... didn't... I didn't kill them."

"Who didn't you kill, Tom?" I yelled.

"My mom and my sister. I didn't do it. It was... an accident. You must know this."

"What was an accident?"

"My... sister... we were playing a game.... She fell and got a rope somehow wrapped around her neck. I took her down and tried to... tried to breathe life into her again. But it was too late.

My mom saw it and thought I had strangled her. She took the blame and went to jail. It was... I didn't... my mom shot herself. The police thought it was me because it was my gun. But she took it when she was at my house. She must have. I didn't... kill her. The blood on the shirt was from a fight I was in, that I didn't want my wife to know about. I went on a bender, that's my crime. I got drunk and got myself into a fight."

Tom closed his eyes and stopped breathing.

"Tom, for crying out loud, don't die on me!" I yelled. "Tom!"

I slapped his cheek, and he woke up again. He looked at me.

"I had... to run away. Raina was gone with the children, and the police were breathing down my neck. I went to Canada to hide. The guy, the real Sean Andersson, was sick with cancer, and I lived with him for some time. I helped him in his garden in exchange for a room for a few weeks. He died, and I took his identity. I buried him, so no one would report him dead. I wanted to continue living as him. I didn't kill him. You must understand this...."

I took his hand in mine and nodded. "It's okay, Tom. You can tell us everything later. We're almost there. We're...."

He exhaled a ragged breath. His hand in mine grew limp. My heart dropped. I could see the rooftop landing spot on the hospital ahead. The pilot was already beginning to descend, but Tom wasn't moving.

Neither was he breathing.

"Tom? Hold on for me. Tom? TOM?"

But it was too late. He was gone.

Epilogue
ONE WEEK LATER

"THE REAL QUESTION HERE IS, was it genetic or circumstantial?"

The lobby of Orlando Airport was crowded. Lots of noise and people going back and forth. Alex and I were drinking coffee, sitting in the lounge chairs in the center of the airport by the check-in.

"You mean, did Noah become a killer because of what they did to him, or was he born that way?" I asked.

"Exactly. Can anyone really be born evil?" Alex said, looking clever and sipping his cup. He tried to hide it, but I could tell he was still shaken up pretty badly after what had happened to him.

"I don't believe that," I said. "I believe there is good in everyone. But then I look at the world and see so much evil out there, dads killing their wives and children just so they can be with their lovers. There are monsters walking around out there, and it terrifies me to send my children into this world. But at least now, Noah will serve life in jail for killing his sister and Dr. Milton. They found surveillance footage from the neighbor's RING that showed him entering his house and coming back out shortly after, at the time he was murdered. He has also admitted to having killed

Trevor, Meg's boyfriend. He tried to pin the murder on Trevor by telling me about the knife, and when he called his dad, he just wanted to find him but regretted it afterward and hung up. He had never spoken with him before."

"He is one sick young man; that's for sure. Hopefully, he will get what he deserves and be kept off our streets," Alex said, then smiled. He leaned forward and took my hand in his. "I never thanked you for saving my life."

"That?" I said with a scoff. "That was nothing. I care about you."

He nodded again. "Yes, you do. Just not enough."

"What is that supposed to mean?"

"It means I will be going to Washington now, and I won't come back. I have enough for my book, and I think it will be very interesting."

I paused. "So, that's it?"

"Yeah, I think it's for the best. Being around you is a lot. It's too intense for me, Eva Rae, and I was a war correspondent. Being around you is simply too dangerous."

That made me laugh. "You're crazy."

He smiled, but it wasn't a happy smile. "That may be, but I'm not crazy enough to try and make you love me."

"What do you mean?"

He leaned forward again and placed a hand on my shoulder, forcing me to look into his eyes.

"I'm telling you this with the best of intentions. You and Matt belong together; it's obvious to everyone. And I am not the man who will get between that."

He kissed my forehead, then threw his empty coffee cup in the trash. "I should go. It's been... well, it's been a trip, Eva Rae. I'll see you around."

He grabbed his messenger bag and swung it over his shoulder, then winked at me and turned on his heel with a quick wave.

"Take care of yourself."

I rose to my feet, heart pounding in my chest.

"But I don't want to be with him. He drives me nuts."

He lifted his arm to wave again, then yelled, "Yes, you do. Goodbye, Eva Rae."

I stood back, feeling like a child who had just lost his candy. Alex was my sweet spot, my icing on the cake, and now he was gone. Where would I go from there?

I had no idea.

I shrugged and threw out my cup. It landed next to Alex's in the trash can.

I guess I was going home.

THE END

Afterword

Dear Reader,

Thank you for purchasing *You Better Run* (Eva Rae Thomas #11). The idea for this book came to me as I was driving my car and listening to the song by Girl in Red called *Dead Girl in the Pool*. It tells the story of someone waking up in the morning after a party and realizing there's a dead girl in the pool, and then she goes on to sing, *I'm the dead girl in the pool*. That started me thinking. What if that really happened, and the girl you pulled out looked just like yourself?

I'm not normal; I know that. But that's how my brain works. Now, that whole story about twins being experimented on actually came from something I read that happened in real life—twins that were separated at birth in the name of science. You can read about it here:

https://www.thatslife.com.au/twins-horror-separated-at-birth-for-a-cruel-experiment

As always, I thank you for your support, and don't forget to leave a review if you are able to.

Take care,

Willow

About the Author

Willow Rose is a multi-million-copy best-selling Author and an Amazon ALL-star Author of more than 80 novels.

Several of her books have reached the top 10 of ALL books on Amazon in the US, UK, and Canada. She has sold more than three million books all over the world.

She writes Mystery, Thriller, Paranormal, Romance, Suspense, Horror, Supernatural thrillers, and Fantasy.

Willow's books are fast-paced, nail-biting, page-turners with twists you won't see coming. That's why her fans call her The Queen of Scream.

Willow lives on Florida's Space Coast with her husband and two daughters. When she is not writing or reading, you will find her surfing and watch the dolphins play in the waves of the Atlantic Ocean.

Join Willow Rose's VIP Newsletter to get exclusive updates about New Releases, Giveaways, and FREE ebooks.
Just scan this QR code with your phone and click on the link:

SCAN ME

Win a waterproof Kindle e-reader or a $125 Amazon giftcard!
Just become a member of my Facebook group **WILLOW ROSE - MYSTERY SERIES.**
Every time we pass 1000 new members, we'll randomly select a winner from all the entries.

To enter go here:
https://www.facebook.com/groups/1921072668197253

Tired of too many emails? Text the word: "willowrose" to 31996 to sign up to Willow's VIP text List to get a text alert with news about New Releases, Giveaways, Bargains and Free books from Willow.

FOLLOW WILLOW ROSE ON BOOKBUB HERE:
HTTPS://WWW.BOOKBUB.COM/AUTHORS/WILLOW-ROSE

Follow Willow on BookBub

Connect with Willow online:
https://www.facebook.com/willowredrose
https://twitter.com/madamwillowrose
http://www.goodreads.com/author/show/4804769.Willow_Rose
https://www.willow-rose.net
Mail to: contact@willow-rose.net

CPSIA information can be obtained
at www.ICGtesting.com
Printed in the USA
LVHW100207270622
722178LV00004B/51

9 781954 938359